Star Shining
Brightly

Louise,

Be A Shining Star.

Marcia & Michel

Star Shining Brightly

Marcia Argueta Mickelson

Bonneville Books
Springville, Utah

ISBN 13: 978-1-55517-909-6
ISBN 10: 1-55517-909-6

Published by Bonneville Books, an imprint of Cedar Fort, Inc., 925 N. Main, Springville, UT, 84663
Distributed by Cedar Fort, Inc., www.cedarfort.com

Library of Congress Cataloging-in-Publication Data

Mickelson, Marcia Argueta.
 Star shining brightly / by Marcia Argueta Mickelson.
   p. cm.
 ISBN 1-55517-909-6 (pbk. : alk. paper)
 1. Women motion picture producers and directors--Fiction. I. Title.

PS3613.I354S73 2006
813'.6--dc22

                                      2006013625

Cover design by Nicole Williams
Cover design © 2006 by Lyle Mortimer
Printed in the United States of America

10 9 8 7 6 5 4 3 2 1

Printed on acid-free paper

Dedication

To my husband, Nolan, and my sons, Omar, Diego, and Ruben. The four of you make me want to be a better person.

Acknowledgments

Thank you to everyone at Cedar Fort.

A big thanks goes to my husband, Nolan, who has supported me through my writing endeavors. Thank you for being a devoted husband and father. I think the reason I take pleasure in writing love stories is because I can think of no better emotion to feel in this life. That I owe to you. I love you.

Thank you to my wonderful boys for loving me despite my mind being in a hundred different places at once. Omar, Diego, and Ruben, being your mother will always be my greatest achievement. I'd like to especially thank my sister, Claudia Armann, for editing my novel and taking all the time to notice the small details that needed to be improved. You went above and beyond your sisterly duty. I will always treasure the corrections and encouragement. I can't tell you how much it meant that you liked my book. I value your opinion so much, and the fact that I know you're truly honest in bestowing it made me feel all the more proud that I'd earned your good opinion.

Thanks to my dad, Jose Argueta, who has shown me that anything is possible. Many thanks to my mom, Lidia Corina Argueta, for showing me the love of literature. My writing ability was a direct gift from you. Mom and Dad, you have both done so much for me, and you continue to show me what it means to be devoted and outstanding parents. I wouldn't be anything without you.

Thank you to Kay Urban for being the first to read my manuscript and for helping me believe that others might actually want to read it.

Mark drove through the security gate and down the long road that led to the back of the mansion. The colossal Cape Cod with its sleepy gabled roof and dormer windows on the third floor announced that he was stepping into a new world. A trim boxwood hedge surrounded a velvety green lawn, and camellia bushes and tea roses filled the planting beds alongside the brick terrace. On the other side of the garden, an Olympic-size swimming pool stretched toward the horizon. He had never been near a home of this dimension. Parking his Nissan outside the three-car garage, he then glared at the dented rear door he couldn't afford to fix.

He carried a box of books up the narrow stairs that led to the studio apartment over his new employer's garage. Working for a famous actress like Lauren Olsen would be a dramatic shift from clerking at the law firm. He'd worked as a clerk for Pittman and Jacobs since his freshman year at UCLA. He was now in his final year of law school, and his law advisor had warned him against working the long hours his job demanded. Mark couldn't afford to quit working, and was grateful to have found this job opportunity.

Charlie, Mark's home teaching companion, had been Lauren Olsen's chauffeur for several years. When Charlie had needed to cut his hours back in order to care for his sick wife, Lauren had agreed to Charlie's recommendation and had hired Mark. He hadn't met her yet, having completed the job interview and hiring process through her personal assistant, Kim. He'd been required to sign a confidentiality agreement, promising not to sell any of Lauren's personal information to the media. Kim had also given him the keys to the garage apartment.

He was quite satisfied with the arrangement. He would be working part-time in the evenings; his days would still be free for attending classes, and with living accommodations included, rent would no longer be a concern. Charlie had explained that Mark would have a lot of time to read or study while in the car when he waited for Ms. Olsen. With all that was required of him during his final year of law school, he would not have been able to work his thirty-hour schedule at the law firm. Having to work so many hours during his college and law school years had extended the time it took to earn his degree past the usual eight years. With ten years of school and a two-year mission, he would be over thirty-one by the time he began his career.

After accommodating some of his belongings and bringing up the rest of his suitcases, Mark readied himself for his first night of work. He looked at his watch, and it was almost time to meet Ms. Olsen up front. He grabbed his Advanced Criminal Law textbook and raced down the stairs to wait for her.

★ ★ ★

Lauren took one last look in the full-length mirror, shrugging slightly. Not her best look, but it would have to do. Her blonde hair hung lightly on her shoulders. She applied a plum-colored shade of lipstick and enhanced her dark lashes with mascara. Her strapless black dress was a little shorter than she was comfortable with, just hanging below her upper thigh, but it was absolutely necessary tonight.

Julian would be at Tony's party, and she was not going to neglect the chance of letting him know what he was missing out on. It had been nearly two weeks since Julian broke up with her, and she was still hurting. Thankfully, John had agreed to escort her to the party. Although John was only a friend, he was by far the most handsome man she knew, and seeing her with him was bound to drive Julian crazy. She slipped on her Manolo Blahnik heels and went down the hallway.

She entered the upstairs family room where Danny and Sophie were eating popcorn out of a big bowl with Tara, who had been their nanny for nearly a year now. Lauren had spent the better part of the evening with them, sharing a pizza they had ordered and later bathing and dressing them. Now in their pajamas, with half an hour before bedtime, they were enjoying *Finding Nemo* for probably the twentieth time since they'd bought the DVD.

Lauren smiled and bent down to give each of them a kiss before she left for the night. "You guys be good and go to bed when Tara tells you to." They both nodded and agreed almost too quickly.

"Good night, Mommy. You really look pretty," Sophie said before stuffing a handful of popcorn in her mouth. The five-year-old looked like a younger version of Lauren—the same light complexion and blue eyes.

"Bye, Mom," echoed six-year-old Danny.

"Thanks for everything, Tara. I'll see you tomorrow. I'll pick them up from school. I should be done early."

"Okay. You have a good time. You really do look nice," Tara said.

As she walked down the hallway to the stairs, Lauren thought about how blessed she was. Tara was a wonderful nanny who really loved Lauren's children. She was also a member of the Church, which made Lauren trust her all the more. Although it had been years since Lauren had gone to church, she made it a point to hire only members of the Church to work in her household. She had utilized the Church employment service in hiring Meredith, the housekeeper and cook; Fernando, the groundskeeper; and Charlie, her driver who had recently cut back his hours. Lauren felt secure having surrounded herself and her children with members of the Church whom she trusted.

In Hollywood, it was difficult to find people who could be trusted. Lauren had found that out the hard way. She had met her husband on a movie set. They had been costars, and it had been difficult to deny the chemistry between them. Lauren married Victor after only three months. Their marriage lasted a little over a year, which was not bad by Hollywood standards. In fact, their marriage would have probably lasted another year if she hadn't become pregnant with Danny. Victor had insisted she have an abortion; he hadn't wanted a baby to cramp their lifestyle or affect their careers. Lauren had abandoned many of the standards she had grown up with, but abortion was not something she would have ever considered. Even thinking about that now made her shudder. Danny was the best thing that had ever happened to her until Sophie came along. She couldn't imagine not having them in her life.

Victor had no desire to be a father and had never met his son. In fact, Lauren couldn't remember having seen him since the divorce except on film. After Victor, there had been many others. Then she married Trevor, who was Sophie's father and did a better job of keeping in touch than Victor ever did. Trevor visited Sophie on occasion and tried to maintain a relationship with his daughter, but the relationship between Lauren and him had never worked out. More recently, there was Julian, whom she had also met on a movie set. Although he was a minor character in the movie she had starred in, they hit it off right away. It was only when Julian landed a few leading roles that he began thinking he was too good for Lauren. Their relationship was now over, but Lauren wanted to even the score a little with him first. Thankfully, her good friend, cover model John Prentiss had agreed to be her date that evening.

Lauren stepped out into the warm September night. The silver Mercedes was parked out in front, and Lauren could see the faint shadow of a man in the driver's seat. She figured it was the new driver, Mark, but became annoyed when he remained inside the car. Hadn't Charlie told him he was supposed to open the door for her? Waiting only a moment before she approached the car, Lauren noticed the man hurriedly exiting the car and coming around to her side.

"I'm sorry," he said, opening the door for her. "I was distracted. I didn't see you come out."

Lauren gave him a cursory glance and entered the car, sitting back against the smooth leather interior. He came around to the driver's side and, sitting behind the wheel, he tossed a book he had obviously been reading over to the passenger side.

He turned around to face Lauren. "It's nice to meet you, Ms. Olsen. I'm Mark. Where should I take you this evening?"

"I'm picking up a friend at the Beverly Hills Hotel. Do you know where that is?"

"Yes, ma'am," Mark said, starting the car. He drove down the long driveway that led to the front gate and Stone Canyon Road.

"Don't call me ma'am. You can call me Lauren. All the staff does."

"Yes, ma'am. I mean, Lauren."

Silence encompassed the car for the next few minutes as Mark drove to the appointed destination. Lauren's cell phone rang and she answered with an impatient, "What?

"Hon, it's me. I'm sorry, but I won't be making it tonight." From the sound of John's voice, it was obvious he had been using.

"You're wasted! How could you do this to me?"

"I'm sorry."

"Tonight of all nights. I needed you, John. What am I supposed to do now? One night—you couldn't go one night without getting wasted?"

"I thought I'd be okay, but there is no way I can make it out the door."

Lauren held the phone tightly in her hand, wanting to throw it against the window. "Fine, just take care of yourself. You owe me, John. You owe me big."

"Sorry, hon," he slurred as he hung up the phone.

She let out an exasperated sigh. "Would you stop the car, please?"

Mark pulled the car over as instructed. She sat quietly for a minute, thinking about what to do. She couldn't miss the party; Julian would think it was because she couldn't face him. Lauren was not about to let him win another battle, but she couldn't show up by herself. That would be worse. She spontaneously got out of the car and opened the front door, sliding in next to Mark.

"May I ask you a huge favor?"

Mark furrowed his brow, looking at her curiously. "What is it?"

"My date just canceled on me and I cannot show up to this party by myself. I know it's asking a lot, but would you please just go in with me? We don't have to stay long, maybe an hour—I don't know—but not long. Please, just say yes."

"I guess I can do that, but what kind of party is it?"

"Oh, don't worry. It's above board. I mean, there will be people drinking, but no drugs or anything bad like that."

Mark looked at her dubiously. "I don't know."

"Please."

"I guess so," he said, seeming like he still wasn't sure about the idea.

"Oh, thank you, thank you," Lauren said, realizing for the first time that Mark was very handsome himself. With sandy brown hair, a freshly shaved face, green eyes, and tall trim body, Mark was just the man to produce a little jealousy on Julian's face. She gave him the address of the party and as they drove, she went over in her mind how she wanted the evening to go.

As they approached the club where Tony was throwing his latest party, Lauren started getting nervous. What if everyone saw right through her façade? She winced at Mark's choice of wardrobe, but figured black dress pants and a crisp white shirt could pass. "Just pull up to the valet. Here's some money to tip him," she said, stuffing several twenties into his shirt pocket.

Mark pulled the car in front of the club and a valet attendant quickly opened his door. After climbing out, he came around and opened Lauren's door. She took his arm and held her chin up, smiling broadly for the paparazzi that almost always surrounded any of Tony's parties. As they walked in, loud music blared from seemingly every direction. She could tell that Mark was completely out of his element and felt a little bad for having dragged him into the situation. They mingled with several people that Lauren knew and she introduced Mark as a friend.

At the bar, Lauren chose a glass of Merlot, and asked Mark if he wanted a drink.

"I don't drink. I think you know that," he said.

"They serve nonalcoholic stuff too. They have root beer or Sprite, whatever you want."

Mark shook his head. "I guess I'll have a Sprite."

They sipped on their drinks in silence for a few minutes as Lauren studied the crowds, looking for Julian. She finally spotted him seated at a small table near the back. It irked her to notice that he looked better than ever. His dark locks framed his handsome tanned face, bringing out his best features: the strong jaw, deep-set brown eyes, and that perfect nose are what had first attracted Lauren.

Seated with him was a voluptuous blonde wearing the skimpiest dress Lauren had ever seen—and she had seen skimpy many times before. Julian and the blonde looked very cozy at their table and Lauren winced at the thought of him with the woman, who looked ten years younger than Lauren herself. When she saw Julian and the blonde stand up to walk toward the dance floor, Lauren talked Mark into walking in their direction. Pretending she hadn't noticed Julian, Lauren walked right past him until he reached for her arm, stopping her in midstep.

"Hi, Lauren. I haven't seen you around lately."

"Oh, well. I've been rather busy. How are you?"

Julian gave her one of his famous smiles. "Very good," he said, putting his arm around the blonde woman. "This is Brittany."

Lauren forced a fake smile. "Nice to meet you. And this is Mark," she said, taking his arm.

Julian raised an eyebrow. "Good to meet you," he said, extending a hand.

Mark took his hand. "You too."

"It was good to see you again, Lauren," Julian said, smiling as he led Brittany away.

Lauren waved as they walked past her. Inside, she felt like screaming. Julian was so polite, devoid of any emotion. Did it not hurt him in the least to see her with someone else? Did he not care for her at all? Could he move on that easily? She drank the rest of her wine with one gulp and angrily walked away toward a small table adjacent to the dance floor. Mark followed her and sat down next to her. For the next twenty minutes, Lauren watched as Julian and Brittany danced. It made her sick to watch him. How could she have ever cared for such a vacuous, self-centered man? She could feel Mark's eyes on her and turned toward him.

"So, who is that man?"

"My ex-boyfriend."

"Ah, and I take it that's his new girlfriend?"

Lauren nodded.

Mark turned toward Julian and Brittany, studying them for a moment. "What is she wearing? Do all women in Hollywood dress like that?"

Lauren turned to look at Brittany and then looked down at the dress she herself was wearing. "Some do."

Lauren greeted a few friends and acquaintances she had met on various film sets or other events. Several people stopped by the table to talk to her. She introduced Mark as a friend and tried to keep the conversation light and impersonal.

A former costar, Ryan Trenton, and his date stopped by to talk for a few minutes and then continued toward the dance floor.

Mark's eyes widened after they left. "Wow, wasn't he in that big action film that came out this summer?"

"Yeah, *Flames of Thunder.*"

The excitement in Mark's eyes dimmed as he thought for a moment. "I thought I saw an interview with him. Isn't he married?"

Lauren nodded. "He is."

"But that wasn't his wife, was it?"

"No."

"So, is he divorced now?"

"No."

Mark shook his head. "So, is that how it is in Hollywood?"

"Sometimes, not always," Lauren said, turning her head away from him. He did the same, probably scanning the party to find some other fault with her Hollywood lifestyle. Lauren's eyes followed Julian and Brittany as they took a break from dancing and returned to their table and drinks.

Seated at the small table, Lauren caught a glimpse of Julian with his arm around Brittany. He gave Lauren an amused grin, which instantly angered her. She wondered if Julian had figured everything out about Mark. How could he? Lauren scooted herself a little closer to Mark who was quietly sipping his Sprite. Before she could think twice about it, she slid her hand behind his neck and pulled his face close to hers.

"Please don't be mad," she whispered as she reached her lips to his and kissed him. After only an instant, they both pulled away. "I'm sorry."

"Why did you do that?" he asked.

"I guess that was part of the big favor I was asking you for. Julian was watching and I'm trying to make him jealous. I'm really sorry. I know I'm using you and I definitely crossed the line between employer and employee, and it will never happen again. I just couldn't let the opportunity pass. He was staring right at us."

"I think I'd like to go now if that's okay."

"We can leave now if you want to. I think I got the reaction I wanted."

Mark turned to look at where Julian sat with Brittany. "I think you're right," he said, noticing the anger in Julian's eyes.

They stood to leave and walked past Julian's table. After the valet pulled the Mercedes around, Mark paid the valet attendant and they were on their way home. He silently handed the change back to her.

"No, you keep that in exchange for doing me such a huge favor."

"Oh, no. You don't pay people for doing you a favor. Besides, if you pay me for having kissed you then what does that look like?"

"I guess you're right," she said taking the money and placing it back in her Prada handbag.

Lauren woke up to her alarm, still feeling the effects of the night before. She hadn't drunk that much, but sleep had not come easily as she'd dissected the evening. Saying that she was tired was an understatement. A quick shower helped relieve the tension headache she had woken up with. After dressing in gray wool pants and a low-cut, clingy, black Donna Karan blouse, she went in to wake up the kids. Danny was already awake and lying in his bed. She gave him a kiss on the forehead and hurried him along. Sophie took a little more prodding, but she finally got out of bed when reminded that she could wear her new red shoes. Lauren helped them to dress, and they met Tara in the kitchen, where they all ate breakfast together.

Tara picked up her own backpack and ushered Danny and

Sophie out to the garage. Lauren followed them out and kissed each of the children before helping to strap them into their booster seats. Once again, Lauren was thankful for the ever-trustworthy Tara. She had truly been a lifesaver. The petite twenty-one-year-old had come to California from her home state of Idaho to nanny for Lauren while attending UCLA. Tara had replaced the previous nanny, Gina, who had been tolerable as far as nannies go. But Lauren had found out only too late that Gina had been selling photos and personal details about her life to a local tabloid.

The current arrangement with Tara worked out for every-one. Tara dropped the children off at their private school each morning before heading to campus. She then took turns with Lauren picking them up, depending on each woman's sched-ule for the day. Lauren reminded Tara that she would pick the children up that afternoon and then waved good-bye as Tara backed Lauren's Range Rover out of the garage.

Moments later, Charlie pulled the silver Mercedes out of the garage and met Lauren at the front door. She put her sun-glasses on and relaxed against the comfortable backseat.

Lauren made a quick call to her assistant, Kim, with whom she spoke often during the day. Kim reminded her of some upcoming appointments and promised to call later. After hanging up, she leaned forward in the car to address Charlie. "How's Brenda doing?"

Charlie sighed. "Not so good. I'm taking her in later today to see her oncologist. Mark will be picking you up at the set, if that's okay."

"Of course. You take all the time you need. Just let me know if there's anything I can do."

"Thank you. I appreciate all you've done already."

Lauren leaned back in her seat, wishing there was some-thing she could do to help Charlie. He had been her driver since she could afford one and seeing him suffer at the illness of his wife was difficult. When Charlie had informed her of the illness and explained that he could no longer work the long hours, she had assured him that they would find a solution. She cut his hours so that he was working mostly only mornings, taking her to the set or various other appointments, but had insisted that she would keep his pay the same. He had hesitated to accept her offer, but Lauren was adamant that he should spend as much time with his wife as possible. She didn't want money to be his concern, so she was firm in keeping his pay the same despite the cut in hours. Lauren understood that Charlie had a son on a mission and a daughter in college and needed to continue to support his family financially.

It was at times such as these that Lauren felt like a burden to those around her. If she hadn't received the DUI several months earlier, her driver's license wouldn't have been suspended and she could've driven herself. How many times she had regretted that fateful evening that Nicholas had broken up with her. She had been so upset that she drank until she could barely see straight. It was probably a good thing the police officer had pulled her over or she could have seriously hurt someone or even herself. Lauren hated herself when she thought about what could have happened. When she thought about Danny and Sophie, it made her cringe. How could she have been so irresponsible? Her drinking was certainly under control now. She only drank occasionally at social gatherings and never when upset or depressed. That was when she couldn't stop.

As they neared the studio, she was thankful that today would be a short day. She was meeting with the wardrobe department, who would be fitting and measuring her for costumes. A quick meeting with the director, Gus, and the producer and lunch with her manager, and then she would be done for the day. She was looking forward to being able to pick up the kids from school.

As she allowed herself to relax, she thought about last night and the new driver, Mark. She had made a terrible first impression. What could he possibly think about her? Why had she kissed him? Had it been only to make Julian jealous or was it something more? She wasn't sure, but she was certain that she needed to be more professional the next time she saw him.

When they arrived and were cleared by the security guard, Charlie drove the Mercedes to the lot where she was filming *Monday's Fury,* her new movie. She was very excited about the project and once again felt thankful that she could work in L.A. During the school year, she tried to work only near home, venturing out to other locations occasionally when the kids were off from school and she could take them with her, with the help of her mother or a nanny.

Charlie opened the door for her and she thanked him, offering her best to his wife. "Can you please tell Mark to pick me up at the Ivy? I'll be having lunch with Sol there. Hopefully, we'll be done about two o'clock."

Charlie agreed and proceeded to leave. She was glad that after dropping off the Mercedes at her home he would then be able to spend the remainder of the day with his wife. She had observed Charlie and Brenda on many occasions and admired their relationship. The love and commitment they shared was something that had never been present in her life. How she longed for a true commitment with a man who could really love her and her children.

The morning went as fast as she had hoped and her manager, Sol, picked her up for lunch. They spent nearly two hours talking about upcoming projects and appearances to promote her current movie, *Running in the Rain,* which was playing in theaters and doing well. There had even been talk about a Golden Globe nomination. As they walked out of the restaurant, Lauren put on her sunglasses and quickly spotted several paparazzi camped out across the street. She knew they would be able to get a few shots of her, but she shrugged it off. She had learned to live with it a long time ago. Why should it bother her now?

The silver Mercedes was parked in front and Mark hurried to open the rear door for her. "Thank you," she said just before he closed the door.

He slid into the driver's seat and looked for traffic before he eased out on the street. "How are you today?" he asked cheerfully.

"Fine, thank you. I hope you weren't waiting long," Lauren said, noticing that it was almost half-past two.

"No, it's fine."

"The next stop is Regency School to pick up my kids." She gave him the address and general directions and sat back to retrieve the messages from her cell phone. She had heard it ring several times during lunch, but hadn't picked up. Most of the calls could wait for later, so she only called Kim back. Kim told her about some mail and phone calls she had received. They went over details that Lauren wanted her to take care of and then chatted about recently released photos of her. Nothing sounded negative. So Lauren was glad that no current untrue rumors were circulating about her in the tabloids.

Mark slowed the car down as they approached the entrance of the Regency School. Lauren instructed him to follow a long line of cars that took turns stopping at the front entrance to retrieve children. The Mercedes joined a line of BMWs, Jaguars, and SUVs as children were guided to their appointed cars. Lauren spotted Danny and Sophie, who were led to the car by an aide.

"Mom!" Sophie exclaimed as she slid into the backseat and climbed into her booster seat. "You're picking us up today?"

"Yes, I had a short day today. How was your day?"

"Good, we practiced for our play."

Danny got in and sat next to Sophie. He reached over to hug his mother. "Hey, where's Charlie?" he asked, clearly not recognizing the stranger behind the wheel.

"He had to take Brenda to the doctor. This is Mark. He's going to be driving us sometimes."

Mark turned around to greet the children then proceeded out the exit of the school.

"Hi, Mark. My name is Danny."

"And, I'm Sophie. I'm five now."

Mark laughed. "It's very nice to meet you, Danny and Sophie."

"Mom, can we please go to the fabric store? You promised you would start on my angel costume. The play is tomorrow and I need it."

Lauren chuckled. "Okay, Sophie. We can stop. Mark, there's a craft store just a few miles after this overpass. Could you stop there?"

"Yes, ma'am."

Both of the children giggled.

"I'm sorry. I mean Lauren," Mark said.

During the drive to the craft store, Danny and Sophie took turns filling Lauren in on their day and what they had done. She mostly listened, making only brief comments. Mark pulled up in front of the store and began to get out.

"Mark, you don't have to get out. I can get the door. Will you just do me a favor? In the glove compartment, there's a hat. Will you hand it to me?"

Mark reached over and pulled out a Utah Jazz baseball cap, which he stared at for a moment then handed to Lauren. "Here you go."

She pulled it over her head and replaced her sunglasses. "I usually have to go in disguise. If I get recognized, it just turns into havoc," she explained. "We'll be right back."

"Mom, do I hafta go?" Danny complained. "I don't wanna hafta go in a fabric store!"

"I guess it's okay. Mark, do you mind if he stays here with you?"

Mark smiled. "It's fine. Danny and I will stay in the car and talk about manly things like race cars or video games."

"Cool!" Danny said.

Lauren ushered Sophie into the store and took a basket. They walked toward the fabrics and Sophie touched every bolt of white fabric she saw, designating each the softest fabric ever. They finally agreed on white rayon and a few yards of lace. Lauren also bought some material with which to construct wings. She perused a few more aisles, choosing a couple other things for the angel costume.

Her mother had taught her how to sew when she was in high school and Lauren had always enjoyed it. As a Relief Society president, her mother had been the epitome of craftiness. Her mother could make quilts, dresses, curtains, blankets, and tablecloths. She was proficient in knitting, crocheting, smocking, cross-stitching, and every other craft known to woman. Growing up, Lauren's family was always tight on money. With six kids and a stay-at-home mother, there was never enough money for everything they needed. Most of the kids' clothes had been sewn by their mother. Lauren had always craved store-bought clothes, hating the homemade Sunday dresses that were handed down to her by her sisters. Lauren's mother had insisted that all of the girls learn to sew and in high school, they were making some of their own clothes.

What was so ironic to Lauren was that Sophie craved the homemade dresses of her friends from church, instead of the designer clothes Lauren bought for her. When she was a little girl, Lauren would have loved some of the clothes that Sophie wore, instead of the pitiful homemade dresses her mother had made her wear. Lauren made Sophie a dress once in a while, but had to repeatedly explain that she didn't have as much time as some of the other mothers to make homemade dresses.

She rarely used her sewing machine anymore, but Sophie had begged for Lauren to make her a homemade costume, so Lauren had agreed. Stepping into a fabric-and-craft store after so many years renewed her love of sewing and Lauren bought an assortment of other items she probably would never put to use. After paying for everything, she was thankful that she had gone unrecognized and they hurried back to the car.

"Mom, can we pick up McDonald's on the way home?" Danny asked. "I'm hungry!"

"Not today. Meredith has probably already finished making dinner. It wouldn't be polite if we ate McDonald's after she went through all the trouble of fixing dinner for us.

We'll plan it ahead of time and do it another day, okay?"

"Oh, Mom!"

"Danny, I promise. We'll do it another day."

Danny folded his arms and frowned. "Well, can we go to the park for a little while?"

"Sophie, do you want to go to the park?" Lauren asked.

"Yeah, the one that Tara takes us to by the church."

"Okay," Lauren said. She gave Mark directions and he drove them. As soon as he pulled into a spot at the park, Sophie and Danny bolted out of the car and ran to the swings.

Mark opened Lauren's door and she stepped out, still wearing her Jazz hat and sunglasses. "We'll probably stay about an hour or so."

"No problem," Mark said. "Do you want me to just stay in the car?"

"Whatever you like," she said. Before walking toward the swings to meet the children, she turned to face him. "I'm truly sorry about last night. I never should have kissed you. I can assure you it will not happen again. It was dumb, really, trying to make Julian jealous. He's not even worth it. I don't know why I did it."

Mark gave her a half smile. "It's okay. Don't worry about it."

"Thanks," she said as she walked toward Danny and Sophie, who were both calling out to be pushed.

Lauren was exhausted after she got home. For a short day, it had certainly been everything but. After dinner, she played in the family room with the kids before getting them ready for bed. She spent the next several hours sewing Sophie's costume. It had been a long time since she'd used her sewing machine and there were several seams that were less than perfect, but by midnight, she was ready to go to bed.

The next day, Lauren hurried to put the finishing touches on Sophie's costume and placed a glittery halo she'd bought at a costume store on her head. "Danny, let's go. We don't want to be late," she called, picking up her purse and Sophie's wings simultaneously. They all hurried down the stairs and outside to find Mark waiting by the car.

She smiled a greeting as she shuffled the kids into the car and followed them into the backseat. The ride to the Regency School was noisy as Lauren went over Sophie's lines with her and had Danny practice the song his class would sing at the end of the performance.

As Mark entered the parking lot, Lauren noticed couples walking toward the school's entrance. Being a single mother was really hard on nights like these. She hated coming to school functions on her own. The school was filled with snobby couples who Lauren felt looked down at her and sought the chance to put her in her place with glances of disdain.

Kim used to accompany her to these events sometimes. But now she was engaged and spent most nights with her fiancée. Tara had wanted to come, but had previously agreed to teach a class at Enrichment.

Lauren impulsively put her hand on Mark's shoulder as he stopped the car. "Will you come in with me? I hate going to these things by myself. All the parents just glare at me."

"Well," Mark said, hesitating. "I guess I can."

The foursome walked hurriedly into the building. Lauren fastened on Sophie's wings and then ushered them into the backstage area of the auditorium. She led Mark to a nearly empty row where they each took a seat.

"Thanks for coming in with me. Kim used to come with me to things like this, but now that she's engaged, I hardly see her. I'm lucky to get her on the phone a few times a day."

"It's no problem. I would probably just have sat in the car reading. It's not every day I get to see angels on stage."

Lauren laughed. "So, what is it you read?"

"Law textbooks mostly."

"So, when do you finish?"

"This is my last year, then I take the bar and hopefully start practicing."

"And then you'll leave me?"

"I guess so."

"That's okay. Hopefully, I'll have my driver's license back by then and I can start driving myself again."

He nodded.

Lauren sighed. He probably thought she was such a loser. A single mother with children from two different men who lost her license from driving drunk. Who was she kidding? She *was* a loser. It had never been so blatant as it was that moment as she sat next to Mark. He was educated and smart. Kim had reviewed all the resumes and thoroughly interviewed each applicant. Mark was a returned missionary, from what Kim had told her, with impeccable references and the nicest eyes. Charlie's recommendation had helped, of course. Lauren had left the decision to Kim and, so far, it seemed like a good one.

The lights dimmed and the performance began. Each class took a turn presenting a skit, dance number, or song. A hearty applause followed the final number.

"Let's go," Lauren said as she made her way down the aisle toward the door.

Mark followed close behind and they found Sophie and Danny leaving the backstage area.

Lauren took each of them by the hand. "You guys were great! The show was so good."

"My angel costume was better than all the other girls'! I told them you made it for me."

Lauren led the kids through the door, Mark which held open for them. "You were the cutest angel, Sophie. And, Danny, you remembered all the words of your song," Lauren said.

"Can we go get ice cream since we did so good?" Danny asked.

"I don't know, honey. It's almost bedtime."

"Please, Mom. Just real quick. Can we?" Danny begged.

"Please, Mommy," Sophie chimed in.

"Okay, okay," Lauren said, getting into the car behind the children.

Mark closed the door behind her and went around to the driver's side. He started the car and pulled out.

"Will you stop at the Baskin-Robbins on Canon Drive?"

"Sure thing," Mark said, merging into traffic.

"Do you want to come in for ice cream, Mark?" Lauren asked.

"I guess I can."

They entered the small shop and Lauren saw that Mark was sure to order his vanilla cone separately. Like most men, he probably didn't want a woman paying for him. Lauren shared a banana split with Sophie while Danny had a brownie sundae. They sat down at a table while the children chattered about their favorite flavors.

"So, you're just a plain vanilla sort of guy?" Lauren asked.

Mark chuckled and licked his cone. "I guess so."

Something about the simplicity of having ice cream with Mark and the kids struck a chord of longing within Lauren. What would it be like to be a part of a regular family with a normal job—or no job at all—and a loving husband? Was she suddenly envious of the lives her sisters led, the lives that had always seemed so boring? A man like Mark would never even consider a woman like her. He was a returned missionary, probably as virtuous and moral as they come.

As they finished the ice cream, Lauren could tell the children were tiring. They stepped toward the exit and Lauren was chagrined to see a familiar scene. Somehow, the paparazzi had found her, probably a tip from one of the ice cream shop employees. They immediately started flashing cameras in their faces and Lauren was enraged.

Mark instinctively stood in front of Lauren and the kids, shielding them from the mass blocking their path to the car. He tried leading them to the car, but everywhere he went there was a camera pointed in their direction. "Will you guys get out of here? Leave her alone!"

Lauren, with a child on either side, picked up Danny, handing him to Mark, and then with Sophie in her arms, turned to one of the photographers she had seen many times before. "Call your guys off, Jonas. I'm with my kids. You know I always pose for you guys. Can you give me a break today? I don't want you guys taking pictures of my kids."

"Come on, Lauren!" a bearded photographer called out.

"One shot of all you together," another one said.

"What's with your new driver, Lauren?"

"Yeah, where's Charlie? This guy's a jerk!"

"One more, Lauren."

"Why don't you guys get a life?" Lauren turned around to say as she got in the car behind her kids.

With everyone safely in the car, Mark maneuvered the car through the crowd and they were finally on their way home. "Does that happen a lot?" he asked.

"Almost every time I go anywhere."

"How did they know where to find you?"

Lauren sighed. "They have eyes everywhere that tip them off for a few bucks. Probably someone at the ice cream store called someone who made a few more calls. Before you know it, they're all waiting for you. It's one of the things I hate about this business. I don't have my privacy and I absolutely hate it when they involve my kids."

"How do they know so much about you?"

"They just make it their business to find out."

"I'm sorry you have to live like that."

"I guess I just get used to it," Lauren said. "It's nice to have fans and people who like your work, but sometimes they feel like they own a piece of you, like your life is their business. That's what I don't like."

As they reached the house, Lauren became aware that both of the children were fast asleep, each leaning their head on one of her shoulders. "They're both asleep. Can you help me carry one of them into the house?"

Mark turned around to look at her and a warm smile spread over his face. "Of course." He came around and picked up Danny, carrying him with one arm under Danny's legs and the other around the boy's shoulders.

Lauren held the smaller Sophie over her shoulder and was able to get the door opened, signaling for Mark to follow her up the stairs. She led him into the upstairs family room, which led to the children's bedrooms. "Danny's room is in there. You can just lay him on the bed. I'll go in there in a few minutes and change him into his pajamas."

Mark did as he was told. Lauren found him in the family room right after. "Thank you," she said, smiling at him.

"You're welcome. How do you get him changed when he's asleep like that?"

"Oh, I manage. I've had a lot of practice. It seems like they fall asleep so easily in the car."

Mark smiled again. She was getting to like his smile.

"Thanks for everything tonight."

"Oh, it was nothing. I was just doing my job," Mark said.

That's right. It was just his job, but for a moment it felt like something more—or maybe Lauren just imagined it. "Thank you anyway. Can you work late tomorrow? There's an event I have to go to."

"Sure, just let me know."

"I'll have Kim call you with all the details."

"All right. Well, good night."

"Good night, Mark."

3

The next morning, Mark hurried out of the garage apartment and into the side entrance of the house into the kitchen. It was empty as usual. Tara had already left with the kids and Charlie had probably picked Lauren up and taken her to whatever appointment she had that morning. He still felt uncomfortable about eating in the kitchen, but Kim had been adamant about his access to the kitchen when she hired him for Lauren. The kitchen was for use by the entire staff to make and eat breakfast and lunch. The dinner made by Meredith was for the family as well as the staff, with the staff eating the meal in the kitchen. Even Meredith had assured him that he could help himself to anything in the refrigerator.

Mark opted for his usual toast and cornflakes. He was

pouring himself a bowl when Lauren walked in. He hadn't meant to stare, but her entrance was completely unexpected. She apparently hadn't left yet—in fact, probably hadn't showered yet either. Lauren was still in her nightgown, a long, but clingy white negligee with only thin straps holding up the low-cut bodice. "I'm sorry. I didn't know anyone was still here."

"That's okay," she said. "You go ahead and eat. I'm just going to make some coffee."

"I can come back later," Mark said, not feeling the least bit comfortable sharing the kitchen with Lauren the way she was dressed. It apparently didn't faze her to be walking around in such a revealing nightgown.

"Mark, it's okay," she said, putting in a clean filter into the coffeemaker. "Let me just turn this on so it starts to brew and I'll go back upstairs to change."

She left quickly and Mark thought maybe she had figured out why he had felt startled by her entrance. He wasn't used to seeing women dressed in their nightgowns, especially beautiful women in sexy nightgowns.

Mark hurriedly finished his breakfast and left quickly, not wanting to run into Lauren again. Taking his backpack from the apartment, Mark drove his Nissan to campus for his morning class.

He reached the house at three after his classes were finished for the day. He went upstairs to do some studying and spent an hour doing an outline for a paper due later in the week in his Comparative Constitutional Law class. Remembering that Lauren had an event that night, Mark felt he should wash the car so it would be ready for the evening. Charlie had told him that the Mercedes should be washed twice a week.

Mark searched the garage for the supplies that Charlie had pointed out to him earlier. He opened the garage door and backed the car out. As he was looking for the outdoor faucet, he caught a glimpse of Lauren sitting in the driveway with a child on either side. He couldn't tell what she was doing because her back was to him, but as he walked around the car he noticed the three of them were playing with sidewalk chalk. As he started soaping up the car, he could hear Danny and Sophie alternately making demands for Lauren to draw one thing or another.

"Mark, come see the trains my mom drew," Danny called out as Mark was about to turn on the water.

As Mark walked over to where they were sitting, he noticed Lauren had drawn a long chain of different colored trains. She was dressed so differently than the other times he had seen her before. Lauren wore faded jeans and a simple white T-shirt, and her hair was pulled up in a ponytail.

"Here's a steam engine! And, over here is Union Pacific and Santa Fe. Those are diesel trains and they're pulling lots of freight cars. Look, Mark. See how long it is!" Danny said, pointing to various trains along the driveway.

"I see. They look good," Mark said crouching down to get a better look at the trains. "That's nice artwork. Your mom did a great job."

Lauren seemed embarrassed by the attention given to her drawings. He was surprised that she would shy away from attention, given her line of work.

"Look over here, Mark," Sophie called from where she sat on the other side of Lauren. "My mom drew me a town. There are different kinds of houses. This one is my favorite. It's got a white picket fence. I drew the tree outside and right here is a little dog."

"That's a great town, Sophie," Mark said, turning to Lauren with a smile. "Nice work."

Lauren shrugged. "They're very demanding when it comes to their trains and towns."

"Are you gonna wash the car, Mark?" Danny asked.

"Yeah, I'd better get back to it," Mark said. "Thanks for showing me your drawings."

"Can I help you wash the car?" Danny asked.

"Me, too," Sophie called out.

"Oh, that's okay," Mark said, not wanting to have Lauren's children involved in helping him with his chore. The last thing she probably wanted her children doing was getting wet and dirty while helping the chauffeur wash the car.

"Mom, can we please help him?" Danny asked.

"Well, I don't want you guys getting in his way."

"We won't get in his way," Sophie said to her mother and then turned to Mark. "Please, Mark."

"Well," Mark said, meeting Lauren's eyes. When she nodded, he said, "Okay, but only if it's really okay with your mom."

"If it's okay with you," Lauren said. "I don't want them getting in your way."

"I think it should be okay," he said.

Danny and Sophie took his cue and began scrambling for sponges inside a bucket of sudsy water. They eagerly went to work, scrubbing the front bumper and license plate. Mark started scrubbing the hood and sides of the car. Together, the three of them had the car completely soapy in a very short time. Mark stood back to survey the progress. Most of the car had been thoroughly scrubbed, so he turned around to look for the hose. He was surprised to see Lauren approach with the hose in hand.

"Danny, make sure you don't get wet," she called out. As Danny looked up at his mother, Lauren pointed the hose at him and splashed him liberally from head to toe.

"Mom!" he cried, laughing uncontrollably.

"My turn, my turn!" Sophie called, running toward her mother. Lauren gladly obliged and turned the hose on her daughter, soaking her completely.

"Now do me again," Danny yelled, jumping up and down.

Mark laughed as he watched the famous movie star in front of him splash and play with her children. He watched Danny and Sophie as they laughed and jumped in the air, begging to be splashed with more water. He was caught completely off guard as Lauren turned the hose on him. She aimed the hose at his chest and quickly turned it up toward his face and he had to shield it with his hands.

As he dodged her aim, Lauren continued to try to soak him. Instinctively, he grabbed for the bucket of soapy water. He picked it up and swung it toward Lauren, soaking her thoroughly. She screamed and dropped the hose.

"You're going to pay!" she yelled as she composed herself and grabbed the hose to once again turn it on him.

Only then he realized the ramifications of his actions. He had just dumped a bucketful of dirty, soapy water on his boss, who just happened to be a beautiful, famous actress.

However, she didn't seem the least bit concerned at being completely drenched. She continued to assault him with the hose as the children laughed and cheered. Somehow, he managed to get out of the line of fire as he grabbed her from behind and tried to pry the hose from her hands. They continued to douse each other as they fought for control of the water. As they scrambled around, Mark's feet got tangled in the length of the hose and he fell backwards, pulling Lauren down with him. She fell down at his side and as their eyes met, she smiled and then burst into laughter. Instantly, the children ran toward them, jumping on their prone bodies and laughing heartily. They all stayed on the ground for several minutes until Mark stood up.

"I'd better rinse off the car before it gets streaks."

Lauren immediately sat up. "I'm sorry that we interrupted your work."

Mark held out an arm to help her up. "Oh, no, you only made it more enjoyable."

Sophie and Danny started tugging at each other as they attempted to take turns spraying the soap off the car.

Once Mark and Lauren were both on their feet again, he saw that she was completely soaked and her face was streaked with dirt from the soapy water he had launched at her. He reached up to clean off a rather large streak of dirt from her cheek. With his thumb, he rubbed her cheek until it was clean. "I can't believe I threw that bucket of water at you. I'm so sorry. You're not going to fire me, are you?" he asked seriously.

Lauren laughed. "No. I had it coming. I started it all and you were only defending yourself. Besides, I don't fire anyone. Look at Kim. She probably works an average of two hours a day because she's so busy planning her wedding, but I'd probably hire her an assistant before I'd fire her." She smiled at him. "I don't fire people," she repeated.

"Thank you," he said. "I'd better dry off the car. What time do you need it ready?"

"About eight," she said, walking toward the children. "Come on, guys. I'd better get you cleaned up. Meredith probably has dinner ready."

The children argued only momentarily before following her into the house.

After getting the children bathed and dressed, she sent them downstairs with Tara to have dinner. Peeling off the layers of wet clothes, Lauren stepped into a tub of bubbles she had filled. As she sank into the hot water, she closed her eyes to relish the moment. The luxurious water relaxed her every muscle and soothed her skin. Her thoughts raced back to that afternoon. Watching Mark wash the car with the children had made her smile. Sophie and Danny had enjoyed sharing the chore with him, something most children did with their dads—something they would probably never get to do again.

Lauren closed her eyes to revisit the image of Mark's tall, lean body bent over the car. She could still feel the impression of his arms around her as they fought for the hose. And she cherished the faint memory of the moment they shared as their eyes met for a split second when lying on the ground. But it had been within an instant of that moment that she'd had a stark realization. She could never have a man like Mark. He was far too good for her and would never want someone like her, someone who had long ago stopped living the standards that were so dear to him.

As she washed her hair and finished her bath, she sighed. There was no point in dwelling on the subject. She would never be able to have a man cherish her and love her children the way she longed for. That kind of man was not available to her; she had ruined that possibility forever. But look at all that she had. She had a career that most women would kill for, one for which she had worked tirelessly for. Her wealth afforded her a comfortable and luxurious home. She could buy anything she wanted. Most of all, she had Sophie and Danny. They were her most precious blessings. Longing for what she could never have would only cause her heartache. In the past, she had thought that she would be able to find love, but it had become painfully obvious that the kind of love that really meant anything would never be found in the places where she was looking.

As she dried off, she walked into her closet and moved hanger after hanger of dresses over, looking for the right one. That night, there was a birthday party for one of her current costars. All of the cast and crew were going to be there, along with many others from Hollywood's most intimate circles. Every dress seemed wrong. She really needed to shine tonight; she had to make herself feel like a star and take away the empty feeling she suddenly had inside. It was a sort of vacuous self-loathing and she wanted it to go away.

She pulled out a short white Versace dress that was completely unforgiving. Pulling the thin straps over her shoulders, she zipped it up and then tugged at the short hem. She would definitely stand out in the dress. Slipping her feet into strappy sandals, she stepped over to her vanity and sat down. A self-deprecating sigh made her realize that no matter how good she looked, she still felt empty inside. Where had that feeling come from?

She spent the next hour drying and styling her hair. Wearing it down over her shoulders made her look younger. She put on a simple silver necklace with a small diamond pendant. Makeup was also kept simple, with only a little blush and lipstick. She surveyed her nails and wondered why she hadn't taken the time to stop for a manicure or call her manicurist to come over. They would have to do, she thought as she filed a couple of nails that had been chipped when she had drawn chalk pictures in the driveway. Lauren hurried to put the finishing touches on herself and picked out a white beaded evening purse. She said good night to the children and spent a few minutes reading a bedtime story to them.

After she did a quick mirror check, she went downstairs. She would be going to the party alone, but tonight it didn't seem to matter like it had the other night. It was an intimate party, mostly close friends and associates. Many of the people from the set were in town working and didn't have dates easily accessible either. Showing up alone did not feel intimidating tonight. Once she got there and was among her friends, it wouldn't matter.

As she stepped outside, only a few minutes after eight, Mark was standing next to the car waiting. His eyes seemed to survey her appearance rather quickly and she wondered what he might think. Was he so proper that he was unfazed by how good she looked? Surely, he was just like any other man; he would've had to have noticed how attractive she was.

"Hi, there," he said as he opened the door for her.

She smiled lamely. He probably thought she was dressed skimpily. Why did she suddenly care? "Hi," she said, stepping into the Mercedes. She gave him the address and picked up her phone. Realizing she hadn't even checked her messages for the day, she spent the next twenty minutes listening to the calls she would have to return the next day.

As Mark pulled up to the club where the party was being held, she realized she was tiring of the same routine. Pull up to the curb, get bombarded by photographers, walk into the party, greet people she didn't even like, drink and make small talk, flirt and laugh, pretending to be amused, go home. It wasn't exciting anymore.

Mark opened the door for her, and she put on her usual

smile. "One hour," she said to him, realizing that was all she could tolerate tonight. As she walked into the club, she was greeted by friends and coworkers.

★ ★ ★

Mark looked at his watch once again. He had twenty minutes before he had to leave to pick Lauren up. Turning back to his textbook, he realized he wasn't much in the mood for reading. He had finished most of the chapter on wills as he sat in the brightly lit parking lot of the 7-Eleven, waiting for the hour to pass. Closing his book, he shut his eyes and rubbed them as he leaned his head back. His mind was on Lauren; she was such a puzzle to him. One minute, she was dressed in jeans and a T-shirt, playing with her children, dousing him with a hose. The next minute, she was squeezed into a tight dress on her way to a nightclub. Who was she really? Which one was the real Lauren?

He was sure that he liked this afternoon's Lauren much better. She had seemed like a real person to him. The time they spent washing the car was genuine. But, the minute she walked outside that evening, it was all gone. The real Lauren, the funny Lauren, the kind Lauren, the beautiful Lauren was gone. What replaced her was a fake, overly made-up Hollywood actress who only seemed beautiful in an artificial, worldly way. Again, he asked himself who was the real Lauren. He couldn't tell, but why did it matter anyway? Come May, he would graduate, hopefully pass the bar on his first try, and find a job. He would leave this bizarre world he had been thrust into.

Mark pulled up in front of the nightclub and was happily surprised to see that Lauren came out almost at the time she had announced. She was laughing hysterically and was clinging to the arm of a man that Mark vaguely recollected having seen in a movie somewhere. Mark hurried to open the door for them and was barely greeted as the couple entered the car.

The man had his arm wrapped tightly around Lauren's shoulder. "Ritz-Carlton Hotel," he said to Mark.

Mark only nodded as he proceeded up the street. It was difficult to ignore what was going on in the backseat. He could hear the man kissing Lauren, and Mark scolded himself for looking in the rearview mirror for an instant. In that instant, he caught a good glimpse of the man kissing Lauren's neck. Mark felt a disgusted resolve to get to the destination quickly and to not look in the rearview mirror again. He stopped at a red light that seemed to be taking forever. Although his eyes were focused on the street in front of him, he could clearly hear the kissing taking place in the backseat. When he pulled up to the hotel, he quickly got out, wanting to remove himself from the scene in the backseat. He wasn't sure if he should open the car door for them or wait until they were finished kissing. Thankfully, the man pushed open the door and walked briskly past him toward the hotel.

Mark had to take a moment to breathe before he sat back in the car. He felt totally repulsed by the actions of a woman he had begun to respect. Maybe it had been his imagination, but he had thought that they had shared a moment after they had fallen to the ground in the struggle for the hose. What had he anticipated? She was a woman of the world. What more could he have expected of her?

Mark climbed back into the car and only glanced at Lauren before driving away. He wondered if she was okay, but hesitated to ask. After all, he was just the driver. It was not his place to delve into her concerns.

He simply drove to the house and opened the door for her. She barely looked at him as she made her way into the house. Mark shook his head as he drove the Mercedes into the garage and went up the stairs to the apartment.

4

Saturday morning, Lauren slept in, not wanting to wake up to the reality of her life. The judgment in Mark's face the previous night had pierced her soul. How was it that he managed to make her feel like nothing with one look? She sat up in bed, trying not to feel the humiliation that had overcome her last night. Why had she allowed Royce to kiss her like that? She hardly knew him, but at the time it seemed like the only way to obtain the solace she desperately needed to soothe her hurting soul. Unable to bear the despondency any further, she got up. A long shower made her feel a little better.

As she was searching her closet, she remembered she had promised to take the kids to the zoo. She sighed as she realized that a day out with Danny and Sophie was probably just what she needed. She chose a pair of casual khaki pants, a black Chanel blouse, and a pair of black ankle boots. Looking at her hands, she knew she was definitely in need of a manicure. After her manicure, they could go to the zoo. She called Kim to make the arrangements, and then went to find the kids lounging in front of the TV in the family room.

"Morning, guys. Did you have breakfast yet?"

"No," Danny said. "After this show."

Lauren went into their rooms to pick out their clothes, and then helped to dress them as they watched the last of their show. They all three went downstairs and the kids ate cereal while Lauren drank her usual cup of coffee.

After breakfast the kids played a video game while Lauren had her nails done. Janice, the manicurist, finished then packed her things up. Lauren looked at her watch and told the kids to get ready to leave in twenty minutes. At 11:30, they met Mark outside. She could barely look at him, feeling like he was judging her every instant.

The drive to the zoo was chaotic as the kids fought over which animals they wanted to see first. Lauren assured them that they would have time to see them all.

As Mark pulled up in the front, Lauren fixed a sun hat on her head and put on her sunglasses, hoping to disguise herself. She did not want anyone to recognize her today.

"Can you come in with us, Mark?" Danny asked, surprising Lauren.

Before Mark could answer, Lauren did. "Not this time, Danny. Mark has a lot of reading to do."

"Reading?" Danny asked.

Mark was about to speak, but Lauren didn't let him.

"He's still in school, Danny, so he has to spend this time reading for his classes."

"Like homework?" Danny asked.

Mark turned around to face the little boy. "Yeah, buddy. Kind of like homework. I usually sit in the car and read my textbooks for my classes while I wait for you guys."

"But you would really like the monkeys," Danny said in an attempt to persuade him.

Lauren knew that Mark would probably have agreed to go in with them if she hadn't objected, but she wasn't in the mood to be in his judgmental presence at the moment. She gathered the children and hurried them into the zoo entrance.

The time at the zoo was pleasant. Danny and Sophie really enjoyed going from exhibit to exhibit, seeing everything from the lions to the elephants. Danny's favorite part was the monkeys, and Sophie kept begging to go back to see the giraffes. They had lunch—hamburgers and fries—at the snack bar. Danny and Sophie also insisted on cotton candy. Several hours later, she called Mark on the cell phone and announced they were ready to be picked up. The Mercedes was parked in front as they came through the exit. The children were excited to tell Mark about all they had seen and their chatter kept the drive home interesting.

After dinner, the kids were ready to unwind. Lauren helped bathe them and the three of them relaxed in the family room watching a video. The children almost immediately fell asleep on the couch as they watched. Lauren took the rare opportunity to read over several scripts that Kim had sent over by courier. She tried to read over as many scripts as Kim had suggested for her, trying to find the right one for her next movie. Eventually, fatigue overcame her, and she carried Danny and Sophie into their rooms and then dragged herself to bed.

The next day, Lauren woke up to help the children get ready for church. She rarely accompanied them, only attending when one of them was involved in the program or had a talk in Primary. However, every Sunday, she awoke to help them get ready for Tara to take to church. Both Danny and Sophie loved going to church and especially enjoyed their Primary classes, but Lauren never felt like going. She knew that her current lifestyle was not accepted by those that did attend and her presence would probably make everyone, including herself, uncomfortable. Instead, she and Kim had regular meetings on Sunday morning. Kim would come over and they would talk about the week's schedule. Together, they would go over the staff's schedule, and Kim would type it up and ensure that each member of Lauren's staff received it, along with pertinent memos. They would talk about news stories, appearances, interviews, new projects, and everything else that needed to be discussed. Lauren went to her office, sipping her coffee, to wait for Kim to arrive.

Kim knocked on Lauren's office door and walked in. She was dressed in her casual Sunday wear, short denim skirt and striped tank top. Lauren wondered if Kim would continue to keep her dark hair in the short pixie style even though she would be getting married in a few months. Kim was also desperately trying to lose ten pounds in order to fit in a smaller-sized wedding gown. She was used to having Kim accompany her most places and drop by the house a few times a day. Now their communication, beside the Sunday meetings, was mostly done through cell phone calls.

Kim dropped her Coach backpack on Lauren's brown leather couch and collapsed. "I can't believe I made it. I've been on the phone for almost two hours with my florist. Can you believe they wouldn't give me a discount on my bouquet even though I'm ordering all my centerpieces through them? You wouldn't believe what a little name-dropping will do. They're big fans of yours, by the way. After I told them that I'm you're assistant, they threw in my bouquet for free. Can you believe that? I think we'll use them for your next party. Is that okay? I kind of told them we probably would. You don't mind, do you? I didn't think you would."

Lauren nodded. "That's fine." She went over and sat next to Kim on the couch, kicking off her sandals.

"So, what's on the agenda for today?" Kim asked. "Oh, I almost forgot. The *Insider.* You'll never believe what they said." Kim reached for her backpack and pulled out a copy of the tabloid. "At least, you're only in the corner of the front cover. J-Lo's got the main spread. I don't know what they're saying about her today." Kim flipped through the magazine and stopped on the page she was looking for. "They're saying that your drinking is out of control. 'Lauren Olsen can't seem to control her drinking lately. Not only has her license been suspended for driving while under the influence, but she has also been seen checking in and out of various rehab facilities. A close friend says that Lauren is dealing with her current circumstances and is trying to stay positive.' I can't believe this garbage. A close friend? What close friend? They're such liars! I can't believe they make you put up with this. One DUI and they make it seem like you're an alcoholic."

Lauren got up from the couch and walked toward the window behind her desk. "I've never even set foot inside rehab." She shook her head. "I don't know why I still have you read those to me. I wish I could be like everyone else and not care—not even read them—but I have to know what they're saying about me. I just have to know. Okay, what else?"

Kim tossed the tabloid aside and pulled out another one. "This one's not so bad. They say you probably will be overlooked for the Oscar nomination. Don't worry about that one. I think you're a shoo-in." Kim turned the pages rapidly. "Oh, no. You're on the 'What were they thinking?' fashion page. What were you thinking? Please promise me you'll never wear that skirt with ankle boots again. Sorry, but it really doesn't look good. I know, I know. You realize that in retrospect."

Lauren walked over to Kim and looked over her shoulder. "It doesn't look that bad," she said.

"Okay. You're right. Not that bad. *People* magazine has a rather flattering picture of you and the kids at the zoo. It came off really good. You look motherly, but sexy. The kids look good too. Good caption, too. Nothing to complain about with that one. The *Redbook* interview came out well. The pictures look good, but I wouldn't have picked this one for the cover." Kim showed her the cover and then leafed through the magazine. "They did well, keeping your quotes in context. It makes you seem likeable. No worries there. Then, there was a blurb about you in *Entertainment* magazine wearing that terrible Jazz hat. I know you wear it for disguise, but I think they've caught on to that one. Even with the sunglasses, they can tell it's you. They don't say anything bad, just a shot of you at the airport. I think it's an old one, though. That's really about it. So, since you're never going to wear those ankle boots again, can I have them? I think they'll look great with this pair of boot-cut jeans I have. I'm wearing them to this barbecue that Alan's family is having."

Lauren sighed. Kim couldn't seem to focus lately. Her mind was constantly on Alan or her upcoming wedding. She wasn't on top of things, which frustrated Lauren, but she tried not to let it bother her too much. There wasn't much that could be done about it anyway. "You can have the boots. It's fine. Have you heard anything more about the *Vanity Fair* interview?"

"No, sorry, but I'll find out tomorrow. Oh, wait. Tomorrow's bad. Alan and I are meeting with several caterers, tasting menu selections, and interviewing the cooks. We'll be busy with that all day long. I promise, on Tuesday I'll find out about *Vanity Fair.* I think we still have time. Have you heard anything about Francesca's? That's the caterer I think we're going with, but we're not sure yet. Alan says they're great, but I told him I wouldn't commit until I taste some of their menu selections. That's a good idea, don't you think?"

Lauren nodded. It seemed that Kim always tried to live like she was in the Hollywood scene. Her fiancé, Alan, was also a personal assistant. He worked for Gregory Grey, an actor whom Lauren had worked with before. In fact, Lauren and Gregory had set them up, at Kim's insistence. They had met once, on the set of Lauren and Gregory's movie, and Kim had ranted about how gorgeous Alan was for weeks until Lauren agreed to set them up.

Now, here they were engaged to be married, planning a wedding that was much too expensive for them. She knew it was more than they could afford, but after hanging around with Lauren so much, Kim had actually started to believe she could live like that too. Lauren paid her well and Kim inherited a lot of Lauren's clothes and accessories. Lauren wondered how much in debt they would be after paying for their lavish wedding. Kim was probably expecting and would likely get a very expensive wedding gift from Lauren. She just wished that Kim would redirect some of her energy back to Lauren's affairs.

They spent the next hour going over the upcoming week, including appointments and employee schedules. After Lauren got Kim talking about work, she almost seemed like the old Kim again. They worked together well, keeping on top of most matters and organizing Lauren's life like a well-oiled machine.

Mark walked into the chapel of what would be his new ward. He had requested that his records be transferred from his previous ward. Now that he was living in the apartment above Lauren's garage, he would have to attend the Westwood First Ward. As he walked down the aisle toward an empty pew, he heard his name called. Mark turned around to see Danny and Sophie seated next to Tara.

"Mark, sit with us," Danny whispered loudly.

Mark smiled and sat next to the eager child. He nodded a greeting to Tara, who smiled broadly.

"Are you in our ward now?" Danny asked.

"I sure am."

"Cool!" Danny said.

Mark smiled at the children, who were dressed so nicely for church. Danny was wearing brown corduroy pants with a white shirt and red tie. Sophie was wearing a blue velvet dress and black dress shoes. Charlie had explained to Mark that Lauren was an inactive member of the Church, but liked to hire members as her personal staff. He had assumed that the children would likely not attend church either, but was pleasantly surprised to see them there. He wondered where

Lauren was and why she hadn't come to church with her kids. Probably just a case of wanting it for your children, but not for yourself. He had seen a lot of that on his mission.

The next day, Mark parked next to the gas pump and filled the tank of the Mercedes. Lauren needed him to take her to an interview after picking her up from the set. He glanced at his watch; he still had enough time to pick her up. Walking toward the convenience store to pay for the gas, he pulled out the credit card Kim had given him to pay for incidentals. As he waited for the clerk to run the credit card, he happened to glance toward a small rack that held magazines, mostly tabloids. Recently, he had seen many magazine covers with Lauren's picture. There was a lot of Golden Globe and Oscar buzz about her current movie, *Running in the Rain.* For some reason, this particular tabloid cover caught his interest; perhaps it was the headline: "Lauren Olsen Moves on to Handsome Chauffeur."

Picking up the magazine, he quickly signed the credit card receipt and paid the clerk for the magazine. Despite the hour, he spent several minutes in the car, reading the article. He was surprised to see pictures of himself with Lauren at the party he had taken her to. There was one shot of them walking arm in arm toward the door and also a close-up of the spontaneous kiss Lauren had given him. The article went on to detail their supposed relationship. Mark was shocked to see that they described many aspects of his life in correct detail. They described him as a Mormon from San Diego who was currently attending UCLA law school and had recently begun working for Lauren. They made hasty conclusions regarding the convenience of his current living situation, located so close to the actress, making their relationship much easier.

Mark shook his head as he finished reading the article. How could they get away with publishing such untruths? Maybe the pictures they had acquired did make it seem like there was something going on, but nothing could be further from the truth. He shuddered to think who would read—and possibly believe—the lies. Would anyone in his family or perhaps from school read it? If someone from his new or previous ward read the article, would they believe that something was going on between him and Lauren? He hated to think about the possibility. Mark tossed the tabloid aside and drove toward Culver City.

As he waited for Lauren to emerge from the set, he couldn't get past the anger he felt regarding the article. How could something like that be written without his consent? His name was used, details about his personal life were described, and false assumptions were made. Would they be able to get away with it?

When Lauren came out, Mark opened the door for her without ceremony, and didn't say anything until they were both in the car. He then turned around to face her. "Have you seen the latest issue of *Hollywood Insider?*"

She shook her head, not looking up from a Palm Pilot she held in her hand. "No, what are they saying about me today. Whatever it is, it won't surprise me."

"Well, it surprised me a lot. I guess it's not just so much what they're saying about you, but what they're saying about me."

Lauren looked up, startled at his outburst. "What is it?"

He held the magazine open to the pages showing the pictures. "How did they get these pictures?"

She shrugged. "Those parties are always crawling with people who take those kinds of shots. Then they sell them to the highest bidder. Tabloid magazines like that use the pictures to their advantage and then just make up a story to go along with it. Whatever sells is their philosophy. Just ignore it," she said, going back to her Palm Pilot.

"Just ignore it?" he asked, disbelieving the lightness she gave to a matter that seemed quite serious to him.

"Yeah, it'll blow over in a few weeks and then no one will be talking about it. Besides, nobody believes what is in the tabloids anyway. It's all garbage. They've never printed one entire truth about me."

Mark was dissatisfied with her attitude. How could she be so blasé about it? "Maybe it doesn't matter to you, but I don't like reading lies about myself. I also don't like the idea of people I know and respect thinking this could be true."

She seemed annoyed by his attitude, closing her Palm Pilot and throwing it in her purse. "It does matter to me, but magazines have been printing lies about me for years, and I just can't let it bother me anymore. If I were upset about every article that the tabloids ever wrote about me, I would spend my entire life angry. Most intelligent people know what tabloids are. They are run by dirty, greedy, ruthless people who don't care that half of what they print is a lie. The people *you* know probably never pick up a tabloid, much less believe anything they read in them. Don't worry about it too much."

He shook his head and then turned around to start the car.

She sighed. "Mark, I'm sorry about what they wrote. I really am sorry that it upset you. You have to know that I never intended this to happen, but there really is no point in worrying about it. Honestly, it will blow over in a couple of weeks."

Mark shrugged, but kept his eyes fixed on the road. Things like this didn't happen to normal people. He was a normal person. How was it that suddenly he had been thrust into this twilight zone where intimate details of your life were displayed in national magazines?

When they reached the restaurant where Lauren was meeting the interviewer, Mark opened the door for her.

She slowly emerged from the car and faced him. "Mark, I'm really sorry about this. I'm sure you're not used to dealing with this sort of thing. It's all my fault, and I'm truly sorry. Please let me know if there's anything I can do to make it up to you." She looked away and sighed. "I never should have kissed you. It was inappropriate and has been the whole cause of this problem. What can I do?" she asked, looking up at him.

He shook his head and looked away. "I guess there's nothing that can be done. I'll just have to be more careful in the future now that I know what I'm dealing with."

She nodded. "Okay. Well, again, I'm really sorry." Lauren forced a smile and then walked into the restaurant.

Mark pulled the car away from the curb and found a place to park. She would call him on the cell phone when she was ready to be picked up.

For the next few weeks, Lauren settled into a routine. She'd wake up with the kids, help them get dressed, and eat a quick breakfast with them before Tara took them to school. Charlie would then drive her to the studio lot in Culver City. Upon arrival, she'd meet with her personal trainer for forty-five minutes, doing a combination of Pilates, weights, and treadmill. It was so much easier to get her exercise in at the studio than at home with so much going on. After a shower, it was straight to hair and makeup and then she'd go to wardrobe, where she was outfitted for the day. Most of her time at the lot was spent filming her current movie. Other times, they'd do rehearsals, run through lines, or meet with Gus, the director. On most days, she'd have lunch on the set. The producers spared no expense with the catering. She usually only had an hour break, which she spent in her dressing room checking in with Kim or making other phone calls. Several more hours of taping followed lunch and then she was picked up by Mark. The kids were usually home by the time she arrived. Lauren would have dinner with Danny and Sophie and then spend some time afterwards talking about their day or playing a game. One or two nights a week, she had an event or appointment in the evening, which Mark usually drove her to.

On Halloween, Lauren made it a point to leave the set early. At home, she put the finishing touches on Sophie's witch costume and helped tie a yellow scarf around Danny's neck to complete his train engineer costume. Danny and Sophie always insisted that Lauren dress up to accompany them trick-or-treating. This was any easy request to comply with since a costume provided for an easy disguise. No one handing out candy that night would ever suspect that it was Lauren Olsen at their door. She quickly changed into her Catwoman costume and donned the precious mask that would save her from recognition.

Lauren led the kids downstairs to where Mark was waiting with the car. Kim had assured Lauren that he had been instructed on Halloween protocol and it had indeed been included in his week's schedule. Until recently, Kim had been Lauren's saving grace. She was the best personal assistant anyone could ask for—always on top of everything and one step ahead of Lauren. That is, until recently, because after Kim's engagement, she started to slack off a little. Lauren couldn't fault her. Kim was excited about her upcoming wedding and was overwhelmed with planning it almost single-handedly. Lauren tried to be understanding by not complaining too much about how neglected she was starting to feel.

Lauren tossed thoughts of Kim aside as she found Mark outside waiting for them. He made a remark about their costumes, and then asked Lauren where to go. She gave him an idea about general neighborhoods, but told him it didn't really matter too much.

The rest of the night, Mark drove them around. He dropped them off at the start of a block. Lauren took the kids and walked with them down to the end of the block where Mark was parked, waiting for them. They continued the routine for over an hour and a half. When Lauren told the kids it was time to go, they both complained, even though their buckets were completely filled with candy. They eventually gave in and Mark drove them home. Despite not being able to trick-or-treat any further, Danny and Sophie were elated with the fruits of their labors.

Danny offered Mark a few Tootsie Rolls, which he accepted. Lauren wondered if she would be able to get the children to bed that night given the amount of sugar they would consume over the next few hours.

At home, Danny and Sophie spent an hour sorting through their candy. It was not easy to get them to relinquish their stash of Kit Kats, Starbursts, and Milk Duds for the night, as they got ready for bed. Over the next few days, Lauren doled out a small amount of candy to each of them, wondering if their huge supply would ever diminish.

★ ★ ★

Mark cringed as he heard the telephone ring. He took a moment to look at the alarm clock. It was 2:30 in the morning. Who would be calling at that hour? It rang a second time and he answered it.

"Mark, I need you to bring the car around," Lauren said.

At this hour? What did she have in mind? Did she expect him to drive her somewhere for a rendezvous? "Right now?"

"Sophie is having stomach pains. I have to get her to the hospital."

"I'll be down in two minutes."

"Thanks," she said, and hung up.

Mark hurried to put his pants on and grabbed a shirt from his closet. He slipped his feet into his shoes without tying the laces and ran down the stairs. He pulled the Mercedes out of the garage and parked in front of the house. Lauren was coming out of the front door with Sophie in her arms and the little girl's hands clasped tightly around her mother's neck.

"Is she okay?" Mark asked, helping them into the car. He hurried to get in and drove toward the gate.

Lauren was close to tears. She clamped a fist to her mouth and shook her head. "I don't know. She woke up at one with a stomachache and I gave her some Pepto, but it got worse and she threw up a few times. Nothing I did seemed to help. It got so bad, she just held her side and I don't know what it is, but she says it really hurts. I'm sorry to wake you, but I don't want to take any chances. I've got to take her in."

"I think you're right," he said, feeling a twinge of guilt for being annoyed when Lauren had woken him up. He sped up, hoping to minimize the amount of time Sophie would be in pain.

"Mommy, it really hurts," he heard Sophie say from the backseat.

"I know, baby. Mark's going to take us to the hospital. The doctor will make it feel better."

Upon entering the ER, Lauren was given several papers to fill out and sign. "Sophie, is it okay if Mark holds you while I fill these out?"

"No, Mommy," Sophie said, clinging harder to Lauren's neck.

"Just for a minute so I can hurry and do this, okay?"

Sophie nodded reluctantly and Mark took the little girl in his arms. She quickly put her arms around his neck and held him tightly, moaning at times.

After the forms were completed, a nurse explained they would be taking blood and urine samples and took Lauren and Sophie into a room. Mark waited in the lobby, not quite sure what to do.

Lauren emerged ten minutes later, her face pale and contorted. "It's her appendix," she said as he rose from the chair to meet her. "They're going to prep her for surgery in a few minutes." She bit her lip and wiped a tear that threatened to fall down her face. "Will you give her a blessing?"

"Of course I will," Mark said, putting his arm on Lauren's shoulder. "Where is she?"

"This way," she said as she started to walk down the corridor.

Mark entered the room where Sophie lay on a hospital bed with an IV placed in her arm. She seemed a little more relaxed, but still held her side. "Are you going to say a prayer on my head?"

Mark nodded as he approached her bed. "Yeah, have you ever had a blessing before?"

"My grandpa gives me one every time I visit him."

Mark smiled and lightly touched her head. Turning to Lauren, he asked, "What's her full name?"

"Sophie Elaine Olsen."

Mark turned back to Sophie and, placing his hands on her head, pronounced her name and then proceeded to bless her with safety and comfort during the surgery. He prayed that the doctors would be alert and competent. He asked that Sophie would feel better soon and that health and happiness would be restored to her. Mark asked for Lauren to be comforted during the surgery. When he finished the blessing, he saw that Lauren had tears streaming down her face.

She wiped the tears and turned her face toward Mark. "Thank you so much."

He wiped the remaining tears away with his thumb. "Anytime."

A nurse and an orderly entered the room and announced that they would be taking Sophie to the operating room. Lauren took a moment to kiss the little girl's forehead and give a few words of encouragement. As soon as Sophie was out of sight, Lauren began sobbing. Mark walked to stand behind her and she turned around to bury her face in his chest.

He stroked Lauren's hair and waited for her to calm down. "She's going to be okay. She's a strong girl."

Lauren nodded and pulled away, looking down the hall as she wiped away more tears. "I just don't know what I would do if something ever happened to her."

"She's in good hands."

"I know. Thank you so much for giving her a blessing," she said, walking toward the door of the room. "Thanks for bringing us. You don't have to wait around. After the surgery, I'm just going to stay here with her, probably most of the day tomorrow too, so I'll just call you when I'm ready to be picked up."

"I'll wait with you, at least until after the surgery so I can see how she is. If that's okay. I wouldn't want you to be alone right now."

Her face relaxed and her eyes glowed, telling him how grateful she was. "I really don't want to be alone. Thank you," she said. "Will you say a prayer with me?"

"Sure, would you like to offer it, or do you want me to?"

She laughed bitterly. "I don't think it would do much good if I said it. I haven't prayed in a long time. I don't think I'm entitled to any blessings right now."

Mark took her hand. "That's not how it works, you know. Heavenly Father listens to every prayer. Just because you haven't done it in a while doesn't mean it's too late to start."

She shrugged. "I know, but can you please say it?"

"I really think you'll feel better if you say the prayer yourself. Let me help you start. Dear Heavenly Father," he said, urging her to continue.

"See, I'd even forgotten that part," she said.

"Go on," he said gently.

Lauren seemed to struggle through the prayer, pausing at several intervals. She prayed for Sophie to feel comforted through the surgery and that the doctors would be blessed as they performed the procedure. Her prayer was short but thorough and Mark felt that it was very sincere.

After the prayer, she seemed more composed and her tears had ceased. They started walking down the corridor and toward the waiting room. From behind a vending machine, a man with a camera appeared and started taking pictures of Lauren. She put her hands to her face, shielding her eyes from the bright flash.

Mark grunted at the photographer and lunged for him, but he moved back out of his reach. How could they do this to her at this moment, in the hospital while she was awaiting her daughter's emergency surgery? He dashed toward the photographer and grabbed the camera with one hard tug, breaking the strap around his neck. Mark opened the camera and pulled out a roll of film, exposing it, and then threw the camera back at the photographer.

"Hey, you can't do that!" the photographer yelled, grasping for his exposed film.

"Get out of here before I call hospital security," Mark said, standing face-to-face with the shorter man.

The photographer cursed and then turned around, walking toward the elevator.

Mark turned around and pulled Lauren into an embrace. "Are you okay?"

She nodded. "Fine. It just amazes me what they'll do for a buck."

"Why don't we find a place where you can get some rest? You must be exhausted."

Lauren shook her head. "No, I'm fine. I just want to wait for Sophie."

"I'll go tell the nurse where we are and ask her to come tell us as soon as the surgery is over. You'll do Sophie more good if you get some rest."

She agreed and Mark informed the nurse they would be waiting in a waiting room that was a little more secluded than the busier lobby. He took a seat on one of the couches and signaled for Lauren to sit next to him. She sat down and eased her head onto his shoulder. He extended his arm around her and allowed her head to rest against his chest. She closed her eyes and soon was breathing evenly, drifting off to sleep. Mark closed his eyes as well and leaned his head on the top of hers. It seemed like the most natural thing in the world to sit next to her, waiting for the outcome of the surgery together. He was glad he was able to offer some comfort to her. She had been so distraught. It was evident how much she loved her children and he admired that aspect of Lauren.

Mark heard a voice as he slowly became aware of his surroundings. He sat up with a start to see Lauren talking with the doctor. He was still a little groggy, but happened to hear that Sophie was out of surgery and sleeping in a recovery room. "So, she's okay?"

Lauren nodded. "The doctor said the surgery went well. They want to keep her here for two days until she recovers a little more. He said she won't likely wake up until tomorrow, but I'm going to stay in her room tonight. Well, I guess it's not tonight anymore. I'm sorry about keeping you up so long. You've got to be exhausted."

Mark rubbed his eyes. "I'm fine. I got some good sleep out here," he said.

She laughed. "Me too. You make a mighty fine pillow."

"I'm glad I could help."

Lauren took his hand. "You helped more than you know. Not just the wonderful blessing and urging me to pray, but your being here with me saved me. I couldn't have made it through without you, Mark. Thank you."

He squeezed her hand. "Yes, you could have made it without me. You're stronger than you give yourself credit for, but I'm glad I could help and I'm so happy Sophie is all right."

"You should go and get whatever little rest you can before you have to go to class."

He nodded and rose from the couch. "I'll be fine."

"I'll call Tara and Kim and catch them up on what's going on. You probably won't have to come back for us until sometime tomorrow."

"Okay, but call me if there's anything I can do in the meantime."

"I will," she said, as she walked alongside him toward the elevator.

★ ★ ★

Lauren made herself as comfortable as she could in the armchair next to Sophie's bed. She was so grateful Sophie was sleeping and was no longer in pain. The tremendous pain Sophie had exhibited was almost too much for Lauren to bear. It had been agonizing to see her daughter suffering so much and not be able to do anything about it. Once again, Lauren felt grateful for Mark's support and kindness. She was thankful she'd had someone to lean on; it would have been excruciating to go through the ordeal alone.

Lauren did manage to sleep a few hours and when she awoke, Sophie was still resting comfortably. Lauren watched her daughter for a few minutes, filled with intense gratitude for the wonderful little girl the Lord had blessed her with. She was ashamed that she had felt unworthy to offer a prayer on Sophie's behalf and was glad Mark had urged her to say it. Why had she felt so inadequate about saying a prayer when, years before, turning to her Heavenly Father had been such a natural thing? Even when she'd first dreamt about being an actress, she had never thought she would stray so far away from the Church. She hadn't meant to turn away.

When she'd first moved to Hollywood, she'd found the local ward and even attended for several months. Then her attendance had become sporadic when she found herself forced to work on Sundays so she could have time off during the week for auditions. Little by little she had eased herself away from the Church, making excuses as to why she couldn't attend. Coming home too tired from work or auditions became her reason for not praying before going to bed. There was no time for scripture study. It had taken several years for her to go from active member to completely inactive. It certainly hadn't been a methodical, premeditated process, but rather a slow development that had happened over time because she had let it. She had allowed other things to become important and had set the gospel aside in order to pursue those goals.

She shut away her momentary thoughts of guilt and stepped

out into the corridor to make a few phone calls, not wanting to wake Sophie. First, she called the set to inform them of her situation, letting them know she wasn't sure when she would be back. She was able to speak to Gus, the director, who assured her that they would focus on scenes that didn't include Lauren. He told her to take as much time as she needed and to keep in touch. Lauren was glad he had made her feel at ease; she would worry about taking care of Sophie and not feel bad for missing work. She then called Kim and asked for a change of clothes for herself, a bag for Sophie with clothes, toys, and her stuffed bear, and some decent food.

After a terrible cup of coffee, Lauren waited for Kim to arrive as Sophie napped. Lauren kept staring at her watch and found herself looking up every time a shadow passed the door. She took the opportunity to make some severely neglected phone calls to her agent and publicist. After her third phone call, she sighed and looked at her watch again. It was past ten o'clock and Kim still hadn't arrived. She was about to place another call to Kim when she heard a light tap at the door. Lauren opened it to find Mark standing outside the hospital room with his hands full of packages and a bouquet of balloons.

"Hi, there," Lauren said.

Mark walked into the room. "How's she feeling?"

"She's sleeping now, but overall, I think she's doing a lot better," Lauren said, closing the door behind him. "You didn't have to come by this morning."

"Well, I wanted to see how Sophie was doing. I was on my way out when I ran into Kim. She sent some things."

"I can't believe her! I told *her* to bring those things. She shouldn't have troubled you with it."

"It's okay, Lauren. I offered. I was on my way here anyway."

Lauren shook her head as she took a few of the bags from Mark. "She's in trouble. I'm really sorry she bothered you with it. You probably have class this morning."

Mark put his hand on Lauren's shoulder. "My class starts in

an hour. Besides, I told you that I offered to bring them here. She was on her way here, but I told her I could do it. Please don't be mad at her."

"Well, thank you. It was nice of you."

Mark set a brown paper bag on the table and then handed her a gym bag and a small backpack. "I think she sent a change of clothes for you and Sophie. I picked up these balloons and some books to keep her busy."

She took the balloons and tied the ribbon to the metal frame of Sophie's bed. "That was really thoughtful of you. She'll be so pleased. Thank you."

Mark smiled as he reached for the brown paper bag. "Here are some breakfast tacos from Don Pepe's. They're my personal favorite. I hope you like tacos."

"Yum, I love breakfast tacos. Thank you so much," she said, taking the bag from him. "You shouldn't have gone to all this trouble."

"It was no trouble at all."

Lauren opened the brown paper bag and found five warm tacos wrapped in aluminum foil. "You're going to have to help me with these. Can you stay for a few minutes and eat with me?"

Mark obliged and they each took a seat at the small table across the room from Sophie's hospital bed. Lauren was so grateful for Mark's thoughtfulness and couldn't exactly voice how touched she felt by his kind gesture. Sharing the simple meal with him brightened her day. After he left, Lauren reflected on how blessed she was to be surrounded by people she could trust and count on.

When Sophie woke up she was delighted by the balloons, and inside one of the bags Mark had brought, she found colored pencils, three coloring books, several storybooks, stickers, and a get well card signed by Mark. That kept Sophie busy after lunch. Lauren spent the rest of the day with Sophie, reading her a few of the books, watching television, and chatting with the doctor.

When Mark came to pick them up the following afternoon, Sophie was feeling much better. At home, Lauren did her best to keep Sophie comfortable. The doctor had given instructions for Sophie to remain home from school for a week, so Tara brought her work home every day and Lauren spent time helping Sophie do her homework.

Lauren checked in with Gus each day, but stayed home with Sophie for the duration of the week. When she finally went back to the set, she felt overwhelmed by Gus's demands. Many of her scenes had fallen behind and although the remainder of the cast was able to shoot some scenes that didn't involve her, it seemed that she spent the entire week making up for the time she had lost. When Friday finally came along, Lauren felt exhausted from the rigorous week she had spent filming.

6

On Sunday, Mark walked into the chapel and was surprised to see Lauren sitting between Danny and Tara. She was wearing a simple taupe dress, the hem resting just below her knee. Mark thought she looked more beautiful than when she was all done up in a fancy dress and makeup.

Danny looked up just as Mark was passing by and in his usual manner whispered, "Mark, sit with us."

Mark obliged and quietly greeted Lauren and Tara. He soon realized why Lauren was there as he glanced at the program, which included Sophie singing a Primary song with the other girls from her class. Although she didn't make church attendance a priority, it was obvious that she loved her children.

After the sacrament hymn, the deacons began passing the

sacrament. Mark was distracted by Danny turning to his mother after she passed the tray without taking a piece of bread.

"Mom, why didn't you take a piece of bread?" he asked.

Lauren looked up to catch Mark's eye and he quickly looked away and tried not to overhear, but it was impossible. "Well, if you don't come to church all the time, you shouldn't eat the bread," she whispered in Danny's ear.

"Why don't you come to church all the time?" he asked.

"Danny, let's talk about this later. Let's be quiet. They're going to bless the water."

Danny nodded then bowed his head, folding his arms neatly.

The duration of the meeting was very spiritual; the first two speakers focused their talks on the Atonement. The youth speaker spent a few minutes sharing her thoughts on Christ's sacrifice. The second speaker was a middle-aged woman who spoke about mercy versus justice. She explained that justice had to be served and our sins had to be made right. The Savior paid the price, through his mercy, to satisfy justice, giving each of us the opportunity to repent of our sins. During Sophie's song, Lauren wiped at the corners of her eyes. It was that image of Lauren that conveyed itself to Mark throughout the rest of the day.

The following day, Mark was waiting in the front with the Mercedes. Kim had given him the week's schedule the night before, and that afternoon he was taking Lauren for a *Vanity Fair* magazine interview and photo shoot. She came outside and slammed the front door shut with her heel as she hung up her cellular phone.

"Kim! I'm going to kill her," Lauren said as she stepped into the car, throwing her phone inside her handbag. "She was supposed to come with me, but her meeting with her wedding planner went long."

"Did you need her to do something?"

"No, she just usually comes with me to these interviews. She makes it a lot easier. I guess I depend on her a lot. I know she has a life of her own, but I'm used to having her around more."

"I'm sure you'll do fine," Mark said, starting the car.

"Wait a minute," Lauren said, opening the door. She got out and walked to the front passenger side door. Opening the door, she slid into the passenger seat. "I'm going to ride up front with you, if that's okay."

"Whatever you'd like," he said, starting toward the gate.

"This is just not my thing, interviews. I get so nervous. Give me lines to memorize, turn the camera on, and I'm your girl. I can do that with no problem, but interviews turn me into a blubbering idiot. I hate not knowing what they're going to ask me, and I never know how to answer. Some of the questions are so personal and a lot of times they twist your words. You end up reading an article and don't remember saying half of those things."

"Well, why do you do it then?"

Lauren laughed. "Because I have to. I wish the only part of my job was the actual acting, but promoting is just as important. If you want your movie to do well, you have to promote so people will want to see it. You have to be out there doing interviews and having your picture taken if you want people to remember you."

"Don't be so nervous. It sounds like you've done this all before, so you'll do great."

Lauren chewed on a fingernail. "Kim always does a good job of calming my nerves. She's always come with me in the past. She just talks and talks about anything, and keeps my mind off the interview. The drive there is always the worst. My stomach gets all into knots," she said, turning to Mark. "Will you just talk to me—about anything? Please, help me keep my mind off it."

Mark nodded. "Okay, well, what should we talk about?"

"Tell me about yourself. Where are you from?"

"San Diego. My parents still live there. I moved up here after my mission."

"Where did you go on your mission?"

"Honduras."

"So, you still speak Spanish?"

"I do."

"Can I ask you a personal question?"

Mark looked at her and was slow to respond. "Um, I guess so."

"Well, I know most returned missionaries are encouraged to marry soon after their missions. And, well, you're a good-looking guy. Do you mind if I ask why you're not married? You've got to be close to thirty, right?"

Mark laughed. "You do get right to the point."

"I'm sorry. I know it's a personal question and you don't have to answer it, but I am curious."

"Well, I am thirty-one. And, yes, most RMs do get married right away. I guess it's a combination of I haven't met the right woman and I would like to finish school first so I will be able to take care of her."

"Take care of her? Most women can take care of themselves these days."

Mark cleared his throat. "I know that. I just don't want to find myself in a situation where I can't afford to take care of my family. After I finish law school and have a higher paying job, I'll feel more secure about being able to get married."

"I can understand that."

"In the meantime, I just have to keep studying, keep my grades up so I can graduate."

"I think you study too much. You always have a textbook at your side."

Mark laughed. "That's what my ex-girlfriend used to say."

"Ex-girlfriend?"

"Yeah, Lisa. She broke up with me about six months ago because she thought I spent too much time studying. She said I never paid attention to her." He shrugged. "Maybe she was right, but between work and school, it was hard to find time to spend with her. I guess marriage is just going to have to wait for me."

"Well, you'll be done soon, right?"

Mark nodded. "Enough about me, tell me about you. How did you get your big start in Hollywood?"

She laughed. "My big start? Well, it was more like several little starts. I had such big ideas about Hollywood when I came from Utah. I thought I was going to be an instant success. Boy, was I surprised. True to what my family warned me about, I was waiting tables within a week and sharing an apartment with, like, five other people. I went to so many auditions, stood in line for countless hours, and couldn't get any work. Finally, about three years after coming out here, I got a break with a one-line part on a soap opera. I guess they were impressed because it became a recurring role and they started writing a story line for my character. I started working consistently and got an agent. My agent helped me get a few more auditions, and for a couple of years, I had little parts in several films. I started getting larger parts and finally got my big break with *A Better Time*. That was my first starring role."

"I remember seeing that. You were good."

"Thanks."

"So, what made you decide to be an actress?"

"I don't know exactly. I guess I just always wanted to be a star. I'm right in the middle of six kids, and growing up, I just kind of seemed to get lost in the shuffle. I wanted to be somebody other than Liesel's little sister or Dave's big sister or one of the Olsen kids. I wanted to be a star shining brightly, shining for the whole world to see." She chuckled. "I never could remember the rest of that Primary song."

"Well, you made it."

"Yeah, I made it," she said with a touch of melancholy in her voice. "I'm a star. Sometimes I just wonder if it was all worth it, you know?"

"Well, is it?"

Lauren shrugged. "I haven't figured that one out yet."

Mark waited for Lauren for two hours and was able to finish the reading for several of his classes. He had come to not mind waiting for her as long as he was able to spend the time on the work his professors had assigned. The previous three years of law school had required a lot of reading, but for some reason this year, it seemed like he spent over four hours a night completing his required reading.

When Lauren came out she was more relaxed, having completed the interview. They spent the drive home talking more personally about their families. Mark was surprised to find out that Lauren came from a relatively normal family. She was vastly different than what he had originally expected of a Hollywood actress.

★ ★ ★

Lauren hurriedly tied Danny's tie and brushed a few specks of lint off his suit coat. She was glad Tara had offered to help Sophie get ready. Usually on Sundays, Lauren remained in her nightgown as she helped the children get ready, but today she was joining them and they were running late as she hurried to ready herself. She zipped up her black knee-high boots and then stood up to straighten her knee-length black skirt. A simple gray formfitting turtleneck sweater kept her look classic. She didn't want to wear anything flamboyant; she already stuck out like a sore thumb and had attracted attention the few times she ventured to church.

They finished getting ready and Tara drove them to the church. Lauren hugged and kissed each child and then released them to join the Primary children and teachers on the stand. As she turned to take a seat next to Tara, she caught a glimpse of Mark sitting a few rows ahead of her. His lips relaxed into a smile and he gave her a subtle wave. She waved back and then sat down, feeling like every set of eyes was on her.

It seemed like just yesterday she was a part of a family like the many she saw seated together in pews around her. Her family always sat in the fourth row from the front, often taking up the entire row. Like most kids growing up in Salt Lake City, she was immersed in the Church. All of her friends were members. Her family was often involved in service projects, always had family home evening, and as the daughter of the bishop and later, stake president, she had lived the gospel. As a child, she had loved Primary and so she encouraged Danny and Sophie to attend. Even as a teenager, Lauren thrived on Personal Progress, earned a Young Womanhood Recognition medallion, and strived to live as the Lord wanted her to. She honored the Young Women values and was considered a good example to her friends.

Somewhere in the middle of her senior year, everything changed. To fulfill a goal for Young Women, she tried out for a school play. That had been a turning point for her. Cast as the lead, Lauren had thrived on the attention she received as the star of the play. Each night of the five performances was filled with euphoria. She had never felt such satisfaction and fulfillment. It was not long after the play ended that Lauren stopped filling out her college applications. It had been understood that Lauren would remain at home and attend the University of Utah, along with several of her good friends from her ward.

Suddenly, college had no appeal for her. She couldn't express it and didn't even try to for a long time. As her friends were receiving their acceptance letters to college, she remained quiet. It was only after most everyone in her class knew their college plans that her mother finally asked why Lauren had yet to hear back. When Lauren had calmly told her mother she had not sent in the application, her mother blew up. She had never seen her mother so upset. Lauren had tried to explain, but her mother wouldn't listen.

Finally when her father came home, the three of them sat down to discuss it. Lauren had explained that she'd decided not to attend college but was going to move to L.A. and get into acting after she graduated. They had tried to dissuade her, telling her that she needed an education. She was too young to be on her own. So many people tried to make it in Hollywood and ended up waiting tables. She knew, however, that it was not their sole concern. Her parents had been more worried that she would easily succumb to the worldly offerings of a Hollywood lifestyle.

Lauren had thanked them for their love and concern but explained that her mind was made up. For the weeks remaining before graduation, everyone had talked to her. Her sisters and brothers had tried to persuade Lauren to stay home. Her bishop, her Young Women leaders, her schoolteachers, her friends had all begged Lauren to reconsider, but she had been adamant. She was going to make it. And she *had* made it. She was a star—but had also paid a price for it.

Now, she sat in sacrament meeting with all eyes on her—or at least that's how she felt. Everyone knew what she was. As the deacons passed the sacrament, she remembered Danny's innocent questions several weeks before. Why couldn't she take the sacrament? Because she wasn't worthy. She had done so many things that made her unworthy. Had it all been worth it? Was she happy with the way her life was? Some aspects of her life—Danny and Sophie—she wouldn't change, but a part deep inside of her longed to be the innocent, virtuous young woman who had vowed to stand as a witness of God at all times, in all things, and in all places.

As she watched her children take the sacrament, Lauren vowed that she would do everything possible to make herself worthy to partake of it as well. She knew it would not be easy, but it was something she had to do for her children, and for herself. As she contemplated the significance of the sacrament during those quiet moments before Bishop Tanner stood up to conduct, Lauren came to a realization that whatever she was going to give up was nothing compared to what she would receive in return.

What was there to give up? The alcohol was no longer pleasurable. It only caused her pain. It had been the reason she no longer had the privilege of driving. She only drank occasionally anymore at social gatherings but it wasn't important. She could give it up, if only to be able to sit next to her son and take the sacrament along with him. The coffee every morning would be a little harder to give up, but she was a disciplined person. She hadn't come this far by doing what was easy. Lauren knew about hard work, and giving up coffee would be difficult, but it wasn't impossible. Giving up men was something she had been contemplating anyway. They only brought her heartache. Her last few relationships had only brought her a minimal amount of joy, which was followed by overwhelming pain, loneliness, and depression. Why should she put herself through that anymore?

As she listened to the speakers that morning, Lauren had resolved within herself to become that person she used to be; the one who worthily partook of the sacrament every Sunday. Although it had been over thirteen years since she had been that woman, she would be her again. Everyone had thought she wouldn't make it as an actress; she had proved them wrong. Now, she had some more proving to do, but this time it was critical.

After sacrament meeting, Lauren praised Danny and Sophie who seemed overcome with joy to have her in church with them. They took off to their classes and Lauren took a moment to sign up for tithing settlement on Bishop Tanner's door before making her way to Sunday School, where she took a seat beside Tara.

That evening when the kids had gone to bed, Lauren took the opportunity to get started on her resolution. She took the garbage can from the kitchen, quickly emptying the refrigerator of the few bottles of wine she kept there. She took several bags of gourmet coffee from the cabinet and dumped those in as well, taking one last whiff of the coffee grounds before doing so. Unplugging the coffee maker and the cappuccino machine, she threw them into the garbage can. It took her a few minutes to find where Meredith kept the plastic garbage bags. She took one into the living room and filled it with bottles and flasks from the liquor cabinet. Running up to her room, she emptied a small stash she kept at her bedside. When she was finished with emptying the house of anything that would keep her from being able to partake of the sacrament, she took three large garbage bags out to the garage. She knew Fernando took out the trash on Monday mornings as soon as he arrived, and Lauren wanted all of that trash out of the house as soon as possible.

Lauren was startled to see Mark open the door of the apartment above the garage. He came down the stairs and stood in front of her. "Hi. I thought I heard a noise down here."

"I was just throwing out some trash."

"Oh, sorry. I wasn't sure what it was," he said, glancing down at the bags she had pushed against the wall. "Did you bring out all this trash?"

"Yeah, I was doing some late-night housecleaning," she said. "Well, good night."

"Good night," he said, smiling at her.

7

On Wednesday afternoon, Mark drove Lauren and the kids to the airport. She did her best to make it home for most holidays and special occasions. They had spent Thanksgiving in Salt Lake City every year since Danny was a baby. It was always a wonderful opportunity to see her family again and have Danny and Sophie get to know their cousins better. Lauren was the only one of her siblings that didn't live near her parents and it was difficult to stay in touch, but she still loved them all. Although they didn't agree with her choices or her lifestyle, she knew they loved her too and accepted her as part of the family. Danny and Sophie loved to visit Grandma and Grandpa, and always hoped for snow when they went there.

Mark pulled up to the curb and took their bags out of the

trunk, giving them to the curbside attendant. The bags were quickly checked in and boarding passes were issued. Danny and Sophie took turns giving Mark a good-bye hug.

"Thanks," Lauren said as she turned to go inside. "Have a good Thanksgiving. Do you have somewhere to go?"

"I'm going to San Diego to spend it with my folks."

"Good. Have a terrific time."

"I hope you have a nice trip," Mark said, waving to Danny and Sophie, who each took a hold of one of Lauren's hands, pulling her inside.

"Bye," she managed to say before she entered the airport. She pulled on a hat and adjusted her sunglasses before going any further. Airports were the worst places to get recognized. As they walked toward the terminal, Lauren felt a sudden anticipation to get to Salt Lake City.

With a new resolve at life, she felt certain that being in Salt Lake would enhance her desire to live righteously. She was anxious to go to Temple Square, which had been a symbol of virtue her entire life. Lauren could remember as a young woman visiting Temple Square, imagining the day she would be married there. What had happened to that girl who desired nothing more than to grow up and become like the women she had been surrounded with her whole life? Why had she deviated so far away from the path that had been mapped out for her from her infancy?

The airplane ride was relatively short and tolerable in first class. Every time the stewardess walked by with the coffee, Lauren's caffeine-withdrawal headache seemed to pound even harder. *How long will this miserable head-throbbing last?* she wondered. But she drank only ice water and shunned the coffee. Lauren's disguise worked well and she wasn't spotted or disturbed. Danny and Sophie kept busy with the new Game Boy games she had bought for them.

When they landed in Salt Lake City, Lauren was able to shed her disguise a little since paparazzi were not common in Utah. Jacob met them at the baggage claim. He was Lauren's youngest brother, a senior in high school, and her favorite sibling. Jacob had always loved "Woren," as he called her when he was four. Since he was so little when she left, there hadn't been any animosity or bitterness about her decision. They had stayed in touch while she lived in California. She had never missed sending him a birthday present and had spent a lot of time with him during her frequent visits home. While her other siblings still harbored hard feelings about her sudden departure and subsequent choices, Jacob had never judged her.

Danny and Sophie also loved Jacob and were thrilled to see him. He joked with them and teased them until they were both laughing uncontrollably. As the bags were loaded into the family's Ford Explorer, Lauren had the children buckle themselves into booster seats that her parents kept in the car for toting grandkids around, and she took the seat in the front. The drive home was spent with Jacob filling her in on recent events in the Olsen family. They made the short drive to South Salt Lake, passing Granite High School where Lauren had graduated. They parked in front of the small Dutch Colonial, the home Lauren had lived in all her life before moving to California. Lauren had offered to buy her parents a new home so many times, but they always refused. They didn't want a fancy house in the newer neighborhoods of Draper. They wanted to stay right where they were.

Lauren and the kids would be staying with her parents, as they always did on visits. Her mother insisted and Lauren happily obliged. She didn't want to stay in a hotel anyway; she preferred being in the home where she had felt so secure during her entire childhood. Danny and Sophie loved their grandparents and seemed to cherish every moment spent in Lauren's childhood home. Jacob was the only remaining member of her family at home, so there was plenty of room. Three of her siblings were married, with children of their own and the second-youngest brother was on a mission.

As they made their way into the home, Lauren was greeted with the scent of homemade apple pies. Joan Olsen always made pies the day before Thanksgiving. As Lauren inhaled the sweet scent, equally sweet memories came flooding back. Memories of rolling out pie dough, and of cooking apples, cherries, and peaches for homemade pies overcame her as she stood in front of her mother.

"Lauren, you look so good, as always. I love what you've done with your hair. I love it. Don't you love it?" Joan Olsen asked Jacob as she walked toward the door and took Lauren in an embrace.

"Hi, Mom. It's good to see you," Lauren responded as she took a good look at her mother. Despite her fifty-four years, Joan still looked beautiful in a classic way. Her dirty blond hair pinned up in a tight bun, her sparkling blue eyes, and skinny frame were enhanced in their beauty by her radiant smile. Dressed in khaki pants and a black turtleneck, she wore a red gingham apron that didn't show even a trace of flour.

Joan dashed to each of the children as she hugged and kissed them. "You two keep getting bigger and bigger every time I see you. I love it."

Danny smiled. "Grandma, can I help you make pies?"

"Me too!" Sophie exclaimed.

"Of course you can," she said, leading them into the kitchen. "And I bet your mom would like to help too."

Lauren smiled and followed them into the kitchen. As the four of them worked on the dozen pies that Joan made every year, the rest of the Olsen clan began to filter in. Dave, the oldest Olsen boy, came in with his wife Amanda and their nine-month-old Nate. Although Dave was the oldest boy, he was several years younger than Lauren. Bob and Joan Olsen had their own version of the Brady Bunch, but with the three girls born first, followed by the three boys. Lauren was happy to see how much Nate had grown in six months. As Dave and Amanda attempted to help, despite following the crawling Nate around the kitchen, they reminisced about the family's annual pie-making tradition.

Lauren's eldest sister, Rachel, arrived next. Rachel had

always been the know-it-all of the family. Taking the role of eldest child very seriously, Rachel never hesitated to tell any of her siblings what she thought they were doing wrong in their lives. Rachel believed it was her duty to dole out advice and lectures whenever any of them deviated from the path she had in mind for them. Rachel was quick to tell Lauren that she shouldn't wear that much makeup. It was bad enough she had to endure long hours with the makeup she wore on the set. Rachel told Lauren that she should allow her skin to breathe on her days off. Lauren ignored Rachel's usual advice and greeted Rachel's husband Jeff, who was followed by their four children. As soon as the four Thompson kids arrived, twelve-year-old Jenny scooped Nate up and ushered the children down to the basement. When the cousins converged, they usually spent their time playing in the finished basement where the television and games were located.

As the adults continued with the pies, they were joined by Lauren's sister Liesel and her husband Matt. Their three children found their way downstairs; the laughter emanating from the basement made it obvious that the children were enjoying themselves. Lauren was especially happy to see Liesel. They were only two years apart and had been the best of friends growing up. Although so many things had changed over the years and Liesel and Rachel were now really close, there was still a bond with Liesel that Lauren cherished. It had taken many years and visits to get to the point she was at with Liesel.

Liesel had been the most hurt when Lauren had decided to go to California. She had felt betrayed by Lauren's decision. As young women, they had often talked about marrying in the temple and living next door to each other, raising their children together to be best friends. Now, Lauren was in California, living a life so different than the one they had planned on, and Liesel was in Salt Lake, raising her family just as they had talked about. It seemed like a lifetime ago that they had made those plans.

It had taken several years for the two sisters to become

friends again, but as Lauren became a mother, she was able to place family on the same high level she once had. Over the years, Lauren spent countless hours on the phone with Liesel, asking for advice about one aspect of parenting or another. As Lauren's visits became more frequent, their relationship improved and Lauren once again felt close to her sister.

Although her family no longer harbored negative feelings toward her, Lauren still felt like an outsider when she visited. They all lived in close proximity to each other and spent immeasurable hours together, while she lived in California and only visited every couple of months. All of her family was active in the Church, and her married siblings had all been sealed in the temple to their spouses. She was different, and although they were all family and loved each other very much, Lauren did not feel like she belonged. As Lauren observed her siblings with their spouses, there was an ache that she had not noticed before when she was with her family. It was an empty-feeling sort of ache. They all had an eternal mate, and she had no one. Perhaps, she had an exciting life as a Hollywood actress and more money than she would ever know what to do with, but she had no one to love her. For some reason, it stood out more to her today than on any other occasion. For some reason, it really mattered today.

Lauren's father came in shortly after that with the Christmas tree. It was an Olsen family tradition that Lauren's father would bring the Christmas tree home on the Wednesday before Thanksgiving and the family would spend the evening decorating it as the pies baked. The commotion from the basement moved upstairs as all the children took turns hanging ornaments on the tree. Lauren watched as Danny and Sophie joined their cousins in decorating the tree. It made her so happy to see them with their cousins, joining in a family tradition that had been so much a part of her.

As the evening progressed, Rachel, Liesel, and Dave all gathered their families to leave. Joan gave out reminders of what each of them was to bring the next day for Thanksgiving dinner. Lauren told each of them how happy she was to see them and walked them to the door. As the crowd thinned out, Joan took Lauren and the kids upstairs and together they helped get Danny and Sophie ready for bed. Joan seemed extremely happy to have Danny and Sophie there and stuck around as Lauren read them a bedtime story and tucked them into bed.

Lauren was happy to gather in the living room with her parents and Jacob as they talked about plans for the next day and shared letters they had each received from Elder Olsen. As her parents and Jacob turned in for the night, Lauren followed suit and quietly went into the room where Danny and Sophie slept. It had been the room she had shared with her two sisters. She took off her clothes and slid in between the sheets of what had used to be Rachel's old bed. Danny and Sophie were sleeping on the bunk beds that Lauren had shared with Liesel.

It seemed like so long ago that she lay in the bottom bunk dreaming about what her life would be like. And now, here she was. She was a star shining brightly in Hollywood. It was what she had wanted, but was it what she wanted *now*? Had all the money and glamour really made her happy? As she thought about how happy her siblings seemed with their little families in Salt Lake, she wondered if she would be happy had she stayed there. At least she didn't have to think about it too long because she soon fell asleep.

The next day was bustling with activity, as was any Thanksgiving Day in the Olsen household. The morning started early with homemade muffins and milk. Joan put the turkey in the oven almost upon awakening, and Lauren was happy to help her with the stuffing and rolls. Rachel had been put in charge of the mashed potatoes and gravy while Liesel was making the vegetables. Dave and Amanda had been given the small assignment of drinks and cranberry sauce.

Joan remained in the kitchen all morning while the rest of the family filtered in. At one o'clock the table had been set and everyone was ready to eat.

Bob took a few minutes to address the family, stating how

grateful he was for everyone. Then he gave the blessing on the food. Lauren thought about how on previous years, she had always inwardly groaned during this part. It was so boring and predictable that her father would take well over five minutes telling everyone how thankful he was for his family. However, this year was different. She was warmed by his comments and even echoed them in her heart. Overcome with emotion, she wondered how she had ever gotten along without her family. As the prayer was finished, Lauren looked around the table at her family, feeling happy to be a part of it.

After dinner, the men retired to the basement to watch the children—or rather, to watch football as the children played.

Lauren stayed upstairs with the other women and cleared away the dishes. Although it never seemed fair that they had to do all the work, Lauren actually enjoyed the girl talk that filled the kitchen.

Friday and Saturday were truly enjoyable; the entire family spent time together, going to Temple Square, ice-skating, playing games, and doing some Christmas shopping. Although Lauren enjoyed the time with her family, she couldn't help feeling like an outsider during their time together.

On Sunday, she finally realized that it was more than just feeling alone. True, she didn't have a significant other to share happy family moments with, but it was not the only reason she felt detached from her family. It became obvious on Sunday as the whole family sat in sacrament meeting. It was unbelievable to Lauren that, in Salt Lake, her entire family managed to find homes in the same ward. So, just as they had when she was a child, they took up the fourth row from the front, as well as the fifth.

On previous visits to Salt Lake, she had refused to attend church, but had allowed Danny and Sophie to go with her family. It was from going with Grandma and Grandpa to church every time they visited that Danny and Sophie had gained a love for it. Lauren remembered that earlier in the year, after an Easter visit with her family, the children had insisted on going to church once they got back home. Thankfully, Tara had volunteered to take them, so Lauren was not forced to go.

This year, however, much to her family's surprise, Lauren agreed to attend church. Nobody was more pleased than Danny and Sophie, for it was the first time she'd gone to church in Salt Lake since her brother's farewell more than a year and a half before. The rest of her family was surprised, but happy to see her in attendance.

During sacrament meeting, she gained an appreciation for her family's strict adherence to the gospel. She was truly touched by the reverence exhibited by her nieces and nephews. It was then that she realized she had made herself an outsider to her family. With stronger resolve than ever, she vowed to make herself worthy. It was this defining thought that pervaded her mind during the trip back to L.A. She felt satisfied with the trip, having enjoyed her family and having made the decision to once again be a true member of it.

Tara dropped Lauren off at the church and took the children back to the house. As Lauren walked inside the meetinghouse, she felt an overwhelming sense of nervousness overcome her. The countless interviews, many auditions, and hours of filming had never brought her such anxiety. Meeting with a bishop for the first time in thirteen years had her stomach in knots. She had signed up for tithing settlement, which she had also not done in thirteen years, and she had asked for a little longer time in order to speak to Bishop Tanner more personally.

She sat in a chair outside Bishop Tanner's office, waiting for him to finish with his current appointment. Opening her purse, she pulled out her checkbook and wrote a check for the amount her accountant had given her that morning. She had asked him for her total year's earnings, including films, guest appearances, and money earned from investments. Now, she was writing a check for ten percent of her earnings, paying a full tithing for the first time since she was a teenager. Taking a moment to fill out a tithing slip, she sealed the envelope and sat back to wait, trying to calm her nerves.

As if she needed anything to add further tension to her night, Mark walked out of the men's restroom and directly toward her. He didn't seem to notice her until he was standing right in front of the bishop's office.

"Hi, Lauren," he said with a question in his eyes.

Lauren shifted in her seat and uncrossed her legs. "Hello."

"Are you waiting for the bishop?"

Lauren nodded. "And you?"

"I'm the assistant financial clerk, just helping with the tithing," he said, opening the door adjacent to Bishop Tanner's office. Inside, another brother Lauren didn't recognize was already seated at the desk. "I'll see you later," he said, closing the door behind him.

Great! Why did she have to run into Mark tonight, of all nights? He probably saw right through her. It seemed to Lauren that he read her every thought, knew her every sin with just one look.

A few minutes later, Bishop Tanner opened his door and wished good night to the middle-aged couple that exited his office. "Sister Olsen, it's so good to see you. Please come in."

Lauren forced a smile and came to her feet. "Hi, Bishop Tanner. Thanks for seeing me." Lauren knew that the bishop was acquainted with most of her story. Her children had been coming to the ward for quite some time.

"Have a seat," he said, welcoming her into his office and motioning to a chair across from his desk.

Lauren slid the envelope across his desk. "I'm here for tithing settlement, but also to talk about a few other things."

The bishop smiled. "Let met give this to the clerks next

door so they can prepare a printout for you to sign. I'll be right back, and then we can talk."

Lauren nodded and unconsciously dug her fingernails into her palms. The last thing she wanted was for Mark to see how much tithing she was paying, but it couldn't be helped. Bishop Tanner came back and smiled.

She had liked this man the few times she'd talked to him before, which made today's task a little easier. "I don't really know where to start. I'm not sure how much you know about me."

"Just start wherever you feel comfortable. If I have any questions, I'll ask," he said.

"Well, I've been inactive since I was eighteen. I grew up in Salt Lake in a really active family, but I left right after high school to move out here and pursue acting. I guess I got caught up in the whole Hollywood scene. I've not been living the Word of Wisdom—basically just alcohol and coffee, but I stopped about two weeks ago and I don't plan on drinking either one of them ever again."

Bishop Tanner nodded. "That's a good decision. I admire you wanting to make a change."

Lauren sighed. "That's not all."

"Go on."

"I haven't been to church regularly since I was a young woman. When I visit my family, I go sometimes. My father blessed both of my children, and I, of course, attended those times. I've gone to my brothers' farewells and homecomings. I've come here a few times for Primary talks or programs, but my church attendance has been very sporadic."

"I assume you want to change that. That's why you're here?"

"I have to change. I've never repented for any of the things I've done. My children deserve to have a mother with integrity. I've put aside the things of the Lord for far too long. I know it's not going to be easy. The things I've done have been so bad. Is there any way for me to come back?"

"Lauren, the Lord loves you. You know that, right?"

She nodded, trying with all her might to hold back the tears that were threatening to emerge.

"He's made it possible, through his Son, for us to be forgiven. If you are willing to put aside your sins, all of them, the Atonement is there for you."

"I really want to."

"The Lord will forgive you if you are truly prepared to repent."

"I am."

"Good. I'm so glad to hear it. Do you have a set of scriptures?"

"In Salt Lake, somewhere, I suppose, but I haven't picked up the scriptures in years."

Bishop Tanner opened his side drawer and pulled out a softcover copy of the *Book of Mormon*. "Here, this is for you. I want you to start tonight, from the beginning. Read every day. I don't know how much time you have, but try to at least read a page—a chapter if you can—every day. After you read, get on your knees and pray. Never miss a day. You should start by asking for forgiveness, asking for his help to forsake your sins. You're right, it won't be easy, but with his help, you can do it."

Lauren dabbed at her eyes with a handkerchief she pulled out of her purse. The bishop's words had touched her so much. She thought she had always known and understood the Atonement, but this time it seemed so real. She could be forgiven for years of inactivity, drinking, and immorality. What she wanted more than anything was to once again be worthy to be at least a fraction of the young woman who had dreamed about marrying in the temple.

"Sister Olsen, you haven't been endowed, right?"

"No."

"These sins are taken more seriously if someone has received their endowment in the temple, since sacred covenants have been broken. Your sins are serious, but they can be worked out." He went on to explain the specific steps she would need to take in order to begin the repentance process. "Let's meet again in a month and see where we go from there."

He also took a moment to read a few scriptures to remind her that the Atonement is for everyone. With a clear, gentle voice, Bishop Tanner read in Isaiah 55:7: "Let the wicked forsake his way, and the unrighteous man his thoughts: and let him return unto the Lord, and he will have mercy upon him; and to our God, for he will abundantly pardon."

Instead of expounding the scripture, the bishop let it stand for itself, its words clear to Lauren that the Lord would pardon her abundantly if she would forsake her sins.

Bishop Tanner flipped through his quadruple combination and turned to Mosiah 4:10, once again reading with a kind voice, "And again, believe that ye must repent of your sins and forsake them, and humble yourselves before God; and ask in sincerity of heart that he would forgive you; and now, if you believe all these things see that ye do them."

He closed his scriptures and looked up to face Lauren. "Heavenly Father loves you. He wants you to ask him with a sincere heart to forgive you. He will do it. Of that, I am certain." Bishop Tanner smiled.

Lauren nodded. "Thank you."

"I'm so happy to have met with you today. Danny and Sophie are wonderful children. They do deserve the best and what you're doing for them will bring all of you true happiness. Heavenly Father loves you and is always mindful of you. Please remember that."

"I will."

"Let me see if they have that printout ready and we can do the tithing settlement." Bishop Tanner stepped away for a minute and was back with a computer printout of the year's donations. He handed it to Lauren and asked her to review it.

It wasn't difficult to review. There was only one donation. She nodded. He asked her if it was a full tithe, had her sign it, and then gave her a copy of it.

Lauren was thankful that the interview was over, but also felt a sense of relief over Bishop Tanner's words. She was determined to do as he had asked. She would turn to the Lord, something she hadn't done for years. She would read her scriptures and ask for forgiveness. Lauren was determined to be the woman and mother the Lord wanted and needed her to be. She shook the bishop's hand and he asked her if there was anything else she wanted to talk about or needed. Lauren shook her head and thanked him once again.

She stepped out of his office and felt a little more composed. She walked further down the hall and pulled out her phone to call Tara. As she dialed the number, she heard a voice from behind.

"Lauren," Mark said, walking toward her.

She stopped dialing and looked up to meet his eyes. "Hi."

"Are you going home?"

"Yes, I was just going to call Tara to pick me up."

"I'm leaving now. I can take you," Mark said.

"That's okay. I know it's your day off."

"Well, it's Tara's day off too, right?"

"Yes, but she was just doing me a favor."

Mark smiled. "I can do you a favor too."

"I know. You've done plenty of them, but really, it's okay. She was planning on picking me up anyway."

"Lauren, I'm leaving right now. Just let me take you home."

She sighed. "Okay, thanks. I'll call Tara and tell her not to worry," Lauren said as she followed Mark out to his car. She called Tara and explained that Mark would be bringing her home. She didn't know why she was surprised to see him approach a Nissan. Of course he wouldn't be driving her Mercedes, but it just seemed odd to go home in his car. Lauren approached the front passenger door and Mark hurried to open it for her. "You don't have to do that," she said.

"I always open the door for ladies," he said.

"Well, thanks." Lauren avoided his eyes. She was certain

that he had seen her tithing check, but why should that bother her? She just wasn't comfortable with him knowing how much money she made. It was also safe to assume Mark knew some of what she was discussing with the bishop. Why should that worry her now?

"It's nice seeing you in church," Mark said as he pulled out of the parking lot.

"It's good to be back."

"Have you been a member all your life?"

Lauren nodded. "But I haven't been active since I graduated from high school. I came to L.A. right after that and stopped going to church. I guess I just got caught up with wanting to make it in Hollywood."

"You did make it."

She laughed. "Yeah, I made it all right, but now thirteen years later, I'm wondering how I deviated so far off the right path."

"Well, it looks like you're back on it, right?"

"I am."

Mark smiled. "If there's anything I can do to help, let me know."

She was really getting to like Mark's smile, and he seemed to dole it out quite frequently. "Thanks. I appreciate all you do for me already."

"Anytime."

That night, after the kids had gone to bed, Lauren began reading in the *Book of Mormon* from the beginning. The first verse hit her like never before. "I, Nephi having been born of goodly parents . . ." Like Nephi, she too had been born of goodly parents and what had she done with that heritage? Just like Laman and Lemuel, she had turned her back on her heritage and refused to partake of the tree of life. As she continued to read and ponder, she saw everything in a whole new light. True and everlasting happiness could only come with and through the gospel of Jesus Christ. The fleeting and temporary joy she'd received through the accolades of her peers and the wealth of her lifestyle had not lasted. They didn't bring her joy anymore, only emptiness.

After reading several chapters, she once again turned to the scripture in the *Book of Mormon* that Bishop Tanner had read to her in his office.

The verse in Mosiah really stood out: "ask in sincerity of heart that he would forgive you." She reread the verse a few more times then went to her knees. She poured her heart to the Lord, begging for his forgiveness and asking for a chance to be redeemed. With a true desire in her heart, she wept for all her past transgressions. She cried as she remembered the drinking, the men, and the greed. Lauren truly wanted to be forgiven of those sins, and she prayed that the Lord would do so. After spending twenty minutes on her knees, she climbed into bed, feeling stiffness in her legs. Although her legs ached from the kneeling position she had been in, she felt the aching in her heart begin to decrease.

Lauren spent the next two weeks immersed in the scriptures. She hadn't read the *Book of Mormon* since seminary, and although she remembered much of it, in some aspects, it was as if she were reading it for the first time. There were so many scriptures that seemed to reach out to her. Each night after she read a chapter, she turned to her Heavenly Father. She wondered how she had survived for so many years without daily communication with Him. Why had she given up the privilege of prayer? On her knees, each night, she asked that He would forgive her for the many sins she had committed. She asked that He would give her the strength to forsake the sins that had become a daily part of her life for years. Lauren thanked the Lord for the wonderful blessing that Sophie and

Danny were and prayed for them. As she lay in bed, she would feel a gentle spirit abide within her. She knew what she was doing was right; she only wondered why it had taken her so long to figure it out.

The first few days were difficult. She replaced her morning coffee with orange juice, and because her alcohol use had been mostly for social occasions, she stayed away from the usual parties and get-togethers. Lunches with her manager or agent were not overly difficult; she opted for diet soda and made it through with no problems. Without feeling the obligation to attend social events, she was able to dedicate more time to her children. She enjoyed the extra time she had to spend at home with Danny and Sophie. She was surprised, but she didn't miss the Hollywood nightlife.

Lauren also spent time preparing for the upcoming Christmas trip to Salt Lake City. There were so many things to do in preparation for the holiday. She was also hosting a Christmas party for her employees, but had left most of the planning to Kim. This caused her some concern because of the upcoming wedding. However, Kim promised to put the wedding plans aside for the time being to dedicate her time to the party. Lauren would have it at her house a few days before going to Salt Lake for the two-day Christmas break the director was allowing.

Lauren managed to find time for Christmas shopping. It was always her desire to personally buy gifts, instead of giving everyone something generic. This year, she was particularly thankful for online shopping. After the kids had gone to bed, she spent hours buying gifts to satisfy her long list, which included Danny and Sophie, her parents, siblings, nieces and nephews, and staff and their children.

Kim helped her do some of the wrapping. Other gifts that she ordered online or bought in town had come wrapped, making her job a little easier. Fernando had brought a seven-foot pine Christmas tree that he set up in the downstairs living room. Lauren and Tara had helped the children decorate it.

The tree was the extent of decorations that Lauren did herself. She hired a company to put up lights outside and decorate the living room and dining room where the holiday party was to be held. The caterers would take care of the food, so all Lauren had to do was get herself and the kids dressed.

The party was held on the nineteenth in the early evening. The following day, Lauren would once again be taking the kids to spend the holiday with her family in Salt Lake. As she pulled on a burgundy blouse over her cream-colored skirt, Lauren thought about how much she was looking forward to the trip. They'd had a wonderful time over Thanksgiving, and Lauren had started to feel once again like a part of her family, much like the time before she had left home.

On previous visits, she had resented their pious outspokenness and the resulting implications, but over Thanksgiving she once again felt like she wanted to be a part of the righteous living exhibited by her family members. She longed to be a part of a family like Liesel's, with a devoted husband and father who lived the gospel.

She slipped her feet into open-toed heels and went into the family room to find Danny and Sophie almost dressed. Danny needed help with his belt and Sophie wanted a French braid. After she finished readying the kids, they went downstairs, where Kim was giving instructions to the caterers.

Lauren laughed as she listened to Kim's instructions. Kim had such a knack for completely dominating a conversation.

In her usual style, Kim thought out loud as she conversed with the caterers. "We probably shouldn't put the entrees out yet, not until everyone gets here. Well, I guess it's okay, just make sure they're kept hot. No, wait. Keep them in the kitchen. We'll bring them out later. Did you bring the sourdough rolls that I asked about on the phone? I think those are the best sourdough rolls I've ever tasted. Are they in the kitchen? Let me follow you in there," Kim said as she ushered the three young women from DeMar's Caterers into the kitchen.

Lauren turned her attention to Danny, who ran over to

the tree, where he had just spotted the newly placed Christmas presents. "Where did all this come from?" he asked.

"Those are presents for all our friends. For Charlie and his family, for Tara, for Meredith and her kids, for Mark, and for Kim."

"Is there anything for me?"

"No, Danny. You know we'll open our presents with Grandma and Grandpa. I'm bringing them on the plane, okay?"

"But Charlie always gets me something," Danny said, looking at the various packages arranged under the tree.

"Well, you won't find it there. Maybe he'll bring something, but don't expect anything. Remember, Brenda's been very sick and maybe they didn't have time. So, please don't ask him, okay, Danny?"

"I won't," Danny said, shuffling his feet as he turned away from the tree.

The doorbell rang and Kim went to answer it. For the next half hour, all of Lauren's staff and their families filtered into the house. Charlie and Brenda were the first to arrive. With grown children who were married, away at college, or on a mission, they were alone. Lauren hadn't seen Brenda for a long time, probably since last year's Christmas party, but she didn't look good. She was wearing a wig, having lost her hair from numerous chemotherapy treatments, and her skin was pale and worn, but her smile was, as always, present. Feeling helpless at not being able to do much to help Charlie, Lauren had given him a larger-than-usual Christmas bonus.

Lauren rushed to greet Charlie and Brenda, inquiring after her health. As they spoke, Meredith, the housekeeper, came in with her three teenage children. Meredith was a widow, but from what Lauren had seen, was a very devoted and loving mother. Lauren always had been impressed with the respect and good manners her children exhibited. Fernando came with his wife, Maria, and their two little children. They were a young couple that struggled financially, since Maria was a stay-at-home mom, but Lauren did her best to compensate him for his hard work. Tara came downstairs and started a conversation with Maria as she picked up one of the toddlers. Mark came in from the garage, unaccompanied. Others attending the party included Kim's fiancé, Lauren's manager Sol and his wife, and a few of the part-time housekeepers who helped Meredith on occasion. Lauren had also invited her publicist, agent, and accountant, all of whom were not able to attend.

They spent the first half hour feasting on shrimp scampi, cuts of baked turkey and roast beef, mashed potatoes, an assortment of salads, and four kinds of bread. Lauren had wanted to keep the menu simple. She had grown tired of attending fancy parties with food that looked anything but edible. The caterers kept the food trays well stocked, and it seemed like everyone enjoyed the food.

After everyone had finished eating the large meal, trays of dessert were brought out. As the guests helped themselves to four different kinds of cheesecake, six-layer chocolate cake, strawberry shortcake, and raspberry parfait, Lauren took a moment to address them and thank them for their hard work and dedication. Next was Danny and Sophie's favorite part as they took turns taking the presents under the tree and giving them to each of the guests. Lauren had bought a gift for each of the staff, along with their spouse and children. Many of the staff had also purchased presents for Danny and Sophie, something which the children also looked forward to every year. Lauren helped Danny and Sophie open a few of their presents as everyone else around them thanked her for the generous gifts.

The guests continued to mingle and sample the many desserts as Lauren helped Sophie open a Barbie that had been given to her by Meredith. Mark approached her and took a seat next to her on the couch.

"Thank you for this," he said, holding a leather briefcase monogrammed with his initials.

Lauren had been very excited to buy that for him. She could picture him walking into a courtroom carrying the elegant briefcase. "Oh, you're welcome. I thought you would be able to use it in a few months to hold all your legal papers and briefs."

He ran his hand over the soft leather. "It's magnificent. I don't know what to say. It's really thoughtful and I can't wait to be able to use it."

She smiled, feeling gratified that he liked her gift. She had been tempted to buy him an expensive watch and so many other things but thought he might feel funny about accepting such extravagant gifts. "I'm glad you like it."

His smile faded as he cleared his throat. He held up the Christmas card that contained his bonus, which she had attached to his gift. "This is too much. I don't know if I can accept it."

"Why?"

"Ten thousand dollars. It's a lot of money. It's really gener-ous, but did you give this much to everyone?"

"No. I give everyone ten thousand for each year they've worked for me. Kim's been with me the longest. Seven years now, so she got the most, except for Charlie. I gave him extra this year because of what he's going through with his wife."

"So, I got the least amount?" he asked.

Lauren nodded. "Well, you've been working for me the least amount of time."

"No, I know. That's okay. I just thought that—well—I didn't know you gave everyone so much. And, well, I was worried that you were giving me a lot more than the others for some reason."

She smiled. He had thought she had given him preferential treatment. If only he knew how much she had wanted to give him. She would have bought him a new car if she had thought he would accept, but she knew that overdoing it would prob-ably offend him. "So, will you accept it?"

He looked down at the card in his hands and then back up to her face. "Yeah, thank you. It's so generous. I'm really grateful."

"I know that I don't always say it, but I really do appreciate everything you do for me. I am so blessed to have all of you help me so much. I don't know what I would ever do without you—and Charlie, and Meredith, Fernando, Kim, and Tara—especially Tara. She loves Danny and Sophie and takes care of them so well. I trust all of you and I need all of you. You guys keep me going. Without you, I wouldn't be able to do anything that I'm doing. Thank you for everything you do. I'm sorry if I don't always say thank you, but I really do appreciate it."

"I'm always happy to help you with anything," Mark said. "I have to say, this was an answer to my prayers. I've been worried about tuition due next week. I wasn't sure how I was going to pay for it, but I guess now I can afford to. Thank you."

"Well, you were an answer to my prayers, though I hadn't been praying," she said with a chuckle. "I didn't know what I was going to do when Charlie's wife got sick. I wanted to give him as much time off as possible to be with her, and at the same time I couldn't drive, and then you came along and solved my problem."

"I guess it worked out for both of us," Mark said. "I know this isn't much, but I have a little something for you and the kids." He handed Lauren three packages.

"Thank you, but didn't Kim tell you?"

"Tell me what?"

"My rule. Anyone can buy the kids a Christmas present, but no one is allowed to buy me anything."

"She didn't tell me, and I'm glad because that's a dumb rule."

She laughed. "Maybe, but I just don't want anyone spending their money on me. I don't want anyone to feel like they have to buy me something."

"That doesn't really seem fair. Maybe everyone wants to buy you something. You should let them if they want to," he said. "Well, I already bought this and I can't take it back, so you might as well open it."

"Don't tell anyone or they'll think I'm giving you preferential treatment," she said with a grin. She fingered the red ribbon on the package Mark handed her. "Thank you. It was nice of you to think of me." She pulled off the ribbon and tore open the wrapping paper to find a leather scripture case with her name on it. Inside was a new quadruple combination.

"I wanted to get you a Louis Vuitton scripture carrier, but apparently he doesn't make them."

She laughed. "No, it's perfect. Thank you." Even if she tried, she wouldn't have been able to think of a more perfect gift. It was exactly what she needed at precisely the right time. His sentimental gesture was almost too much for her to take, and she struggled to keep herself composed. "This is exactly what I need. I was going to buy one when I went to Salt Lake tomorrow, but it means so much more coming from you." As she looked up to meet his eyes, she could feel that he wanted her to embrace the gospel once again. Was it just one member hoping to bring back an inactive member to the Lord's fold, or was it more than that?

"I have a little something for the kids too," he said.

"Danny, Sophie, come here a minute."

The children had been playing on the floor next to her with a few of their new toys. Both children came to her side. Mark gave them each a present, which they tore open vigorously. Sophie's was a small wooden dollhouse that was painted pink with a bright red roof. It had two floors with three rooms on each floor and had windows with red-trimmed shutters.

"Mom, look. I've never seen one like this!" she exclaimed, examining each room. "It looks handmade."

"Did you make that, Mark?" Lauren asked, fingering the smooth, sanded walls.

He nodded.

"It's wonderful. I can't believe you would make this for her."

"I love it, Mark," Sophie said, placing it on her mother's lap as she hugged Mark. She then took the dollhouse and ran across the room to show Tara.

Lauren looked at Mark and felt something deep in her heart. What a kind, intuitive man to make such a fantastic handmade gift for her daughter—something her own father would never think twice about doing. "That's so nice. When did you do this?"

"Over Thanksgiving break. My father has a great shop in his garage."

"Wow!" Danny said as he opened his gift. "Mom, look, it's a model train set and it has a Union Pacific engine and Santa Fe caboose."

Lauren looked over Danny's shoulder to survey his gift. "That great. You don't have any model trains yet."

"Thanks, Mark," Danny said. "Will you help me put it together?"

"Sure, buddy," Mark said, squatting on the floor to help Danny open the package.

As Lauren watched Mark help Danny assemble the train set, she smiled at the image it provoked in her mind. In a dream life, certainly not her own, it looked like a father and son playing together.

Would such an image ever become a reality in her own life? It seemed so doubtful.

She watched them play together for several minutes, and then Danny reached for one unopened present that lay with his other ones.

"Mark, this is for you," he said shyly. "I made it."

Lauren was surprised by Danny's gesture. He hadn't mentioned a gift that he'd made for Mark. She watched as Mark unwrapped the small, awkwardly wrapped gift. It was a hand-painted foam picture frame that held Danny's most recent school picture.

"I made two of them. One is for my mom, but I'm going to give it to her on Christmas."

Mark smiled and patted Danny's shoulder. "Thank you so much. This is a really great frame, and I like your picture. It was nice of you to make it for me."

Danny smiled. "You can put it on your desk or something."

"Sure," Mark said, turning to wink at Lauren.

It warmed her heart to see Danny's gesture and more so to see Mark's genuine response. Although it made her happier than she could say, it also touched her in a bittersweet way. Obviously, Danny felt warmly toward Mark, just as she did, but it would probably never come to anything. It made her heart ache to see her son feeling a longing toward a man who couldn't possibly want to be a part of her life.

The thought ran through her mind more than ever during the holidays spent with her family. Lauren was thrilled to see her brother, who had just returned from his mission. She enjoyed being with her family, and for the first time, she participated completely in the Christmas traditions, going to church with them, attending their ward Christmas party, and caroling during family home evening. The spiritual side of the holiday touched Lauren like never before.

Walking on Temple Square and seeing the lights in the evening was more than she could bear. For the first time in a long time, she felt those temple blessings could one day be hers. She wanted it more than anything and it made her desire to live righteously multiply.

The one difficult part of her trip was once again feeling an emptiness as she watched her siblings interact with their spouses. Could that type of happiness ever be hers? As she prayed each night, she asked Heavenly Father to bless her with the opportunity to experience that kind of love someday. She not only wanted it for herself, but for Danny and Sophie as well. Maybe she didn't deserve it, but they certainly did.

10.

Mark had heard Lauren mention the upcoming Golden Globe Awards and knew she had been nominated for best actress. Because the award ceremony was being held on a Sunday and Lauren gave all the Mormon staff Sundays off in observance of the Sabbath, she had ordered a limo service to take her.

As he sat on the couch near the window of the garage apartment, he saw the limo drive up. It was a sleek, black stretch limousine and the driver promptly got out to stand by it, awaiting the arrival of his client. Minutes later, Lauren appeared in a long, navy blue gown. Her hair had been done up and she was breathtaking. A man walked by her side, and Mark was surprised to see how young he looked. He couldn't be more than twenty-one or twenty-two, but when a woman was that beautiful, she could probably get any man she wanted. Still, Mark felt a stir of bewilderment as they both stepped into the limo and were whisked out of sight.

Mark was more than a little curious to see if Lauren would win and flipped the TV on in an attempt to catch a glimpse of her. As the camera panned the audience, Mark kept his eyes glued to the TV to see if he could spot Lauren. When the Best Actress award was presented, the camera stayed on her for several seconds. Lauren's hand was nervously clutching her date's arm and for a moment, Mark couldn't help but feel jealousy start to creep over him. It surprised him to feel a twinge of envy as he wished it were him seated beside the beautiful actress. He was disappointed to see another actress take home the coveted award. After Lauren's category was announced, he turned the TV off.

The next morning, he awoke at his usual time and after showering and getting dressed, he made his way into the kitchen. His heart froze when he saw Lauren's date from the night before in the kitchen. He was wearing pajamas and whistling as he flipped pancakes at the stove. Mark tried to back out of the kitchen unnoticed but was unable to do so.

The man noticed him right away. "Hi, there. You must be Mark. I'm Rich," he said, walking over to Mark, his hand extended.

A cursory look around the room revealed that Rich was alone. Mark took his hand and shook it. "I didn't mean to interrupt. I'll just go."

"No, man. Come in. I was just making some pancakes. I made way too many, so you have to help me out."

"No, it's okay," Mark said as he took another step back.

"I have almost two dozen pancakes here. The kids will have a few and you know Lauren hardly eats anything. You can't expect me to eat all this."

Mark relaxed at Rich's easygoing nature. None of Lauren's previous dates or boyfriends seemed to have a kind manner like his. "Okay, if you're sure it's all right."

Danny came bounding in, followed by Sophie. "You're making pancakes!" Danny exclaimed.

"Yeah, bud. Come get started before they get cold."

As Danny took a seat at the table, Mark wondered if this were the kids' father. He seemed too young to already have children that age. If he was in fact their father, Mark was very much intruding.

Rich brought a plate of pancakes to the table. "Let's say a blessing first, bud."

"Okay," Danny said, crossing his arms.

Sophie followed suit and Rich said a blessing on the food.

Mark didn't hear a word of the prayer as his mind pondered the situation. After the blessing, Sophie forked an entire pancake, taking a small bite of it. "Uncle Rich makes the best pancakes."

Uncle? Oh, so this was Lauren's *brother*. How could he not have seen the resemblance? He felt so foolish now about the thoughts that had been running through his mind. He had assumed Rich was a boyfriend of some kind who had spent the night with her. How ashamed Mark felt to now learn the truth. Most of the shame was gone from his face when Lauren and Tara came into the kitchen. Mark didn't fail to notice Rich's eyes light up at the sight of Tara.

"You must be Tara," he said, standing up.

Lauren introduced them, and Rich offered them both pancakes. Tara ate quickly and was soon out the door with the kids in tow.

"Why didn't you tell me how pretty she is?" Rich asked after Tara had left.

Lauren laughed. "Sorry."

"She doesn't have a boyfriend, does she?"

Lauren shook her head as she took a sip of orange juice.

"I hope she has the night off tomorrow. You think she'd be willing to show me the sights in L.A.?"

"Probably," Lauren said with a sly grin.

"Well, I'm going to shower. How soon do we leave?" Rich asked.

"As soon as you're ready," she said.

"Nice to meet you, Mark," Rich said, standing up and walking out.

Mark felt uncomfortable about being left alone with Lauren. "I'm sorry you didn't win last night," he said.

"That's okay. I didn't think I would."

He smiled sympathetically. "Your brother seems nice."

"He's the best. I've missed him a lot while he's been on his mission. He came back just before Christmas. He's excited to go down to the set with me today, but from the looks of it, that might be all I see of him while he's here. He seems quite taken with Tara."

Mark chuckled. "Well, I'd better get going. Tell Rich thanks for the pancakes."

"Sure," she said. "You don't have to pick me up today. Rich's going to drive. I'll let you know if we need anything this evening."

"Okay," he said, getting up to leave.

★ ★ ★

Rich enjoyed the day at the set, and Lauren loved to show him around and introduce him to everyone. At home, he and Tara hit it off at dinner and he invited her to a movie. Lauren was happy to see her little brother smitten with the young woman she had come to love.

The rest of Rich's stay was much like the first day. He spent every possible moment with Tara. Lauren didn't mind. She was happy to see the two of them form a friendship.

After Rich's departure, Tara and Rich continued to correspond via e-mail and frequent calls. One evening after Tara had hung up from an hour-long conversation with Rich, she came into the upstairs family room where Lauren was watching a DVD with the kids.

Tara took a seat on the couch beside Lauren and wistfully told her of her conversation with Rich. Tara missed him greatly. Although, they'd only spent a few days together, she had really come to care about him. As Tara talked about her feelings, Lauren came up with an idea.

"What would you say if I gave you an early Valentine's Day present?"

"What do you mean?" Tara asked.

Lauren smiled and reached for the phone. "Kim, I need you to book a flight to Salt Lake City."

"Are you taking the kids?" Kim asked on the phone.

"No. Just one first-class round-trip ticket leaving on Friday, February thirteenth, in the afternoon and coming back on Sunday evening in the name of Tara McGuire."

A gasp erupted from the other end of the room as the realization hit Tara. Lauren continued. "Book a room at the Marriott for Friday and Saturday. Rental car at the airport. I think that should cover it. Thanks, Kim."

"Are you sure?" Tara asked, eyes wide at the possibility of seeing Rich. "It's too much."

"It's a present for Rich too. He really misses you. I wish it could be longer, but you have classes, right?"

Tara nodded. "Thank you, Lauren. That means so much."

"I'm really glad that you guys have hit it off. Let's make it a surprise. Don't tell him anything. I'll make sure my parents keep him at home and you just pick up the rental car and show up on his doorstep. He'll be so shocked."

Tara giggled. "I can't wait."

Lauren felt so happy at the prospect of Rich and Tara together. Valentine's Day came, and Lauren got a call from an elated Rich, who thanked her profusely for sending Tara to Salt Lake. He had been completely surprised to see Tara at the door. Rich told Lauren that *happy* was not a strong enough word to describe how he felt when he saw her. They'd gone out to dinner on Friday and then stayed up late into the night talking. On Saturday, he'd taken her around to meet Liesel, Rachel, and Dave, along with their families. He'd also hastily planned a Valentine's Day date to take Tara to the Roof Restaurant and a concert at Symphony Hall, with a walk on the temple grounds afterwards. Rich thanked Lauren again before hanging up.

She was happy that the surprise had worked and that both Tara and Rich were enjoying each other's company. Hearing their wonderful plans and the excitement in Rich's voice at being able to spend Valentine's Day with someone he was crazy about brought a little envy into her heart. Of course, she was happy for them, but couldn't help but wish there were somebody special in her life too.

After work, she went into her office to put together a few things she had bought for Danny and Sophie for Valentine's Day. They were both in the kitchen waiting for her. Danny was happy to receive a box of chocolates and a ceramic train piggy bank. Sophie was beside herself upon opening new silky white pajamas with hearts all over them and a heart-shaped box of candy.

Once the presents had been put away, Lauren began searching the kitchen cabinets. She had promised them they could make heart-shaped sugar cookies. She couldn't remember the last time she'd made anything, so it took several minutes to locate cookie sheets, flour, sugar, and all of the other ingredients needed. The kids took turns measuring ingredients as Lauren supervised. They each had a ball of dough, which they were kneading and rolling on the counter when Mark walked in.

She couldn't help it—Lauren's pulse seemed to quicken lately anytime she saw Mark. As always, he looked handsome in simple khakis and an off-white button-down shirt.

"Hello," he said, walking in.

"Hi, Mark," Danny said. "Wanna help us make cookies?"

"Danny, he's here to eat dinner."

"After dinner, then?" Danny insisted.

Mark caught Lauren's eyes and she smiled, hoping he could read her mind that it was more than okay. He seemed to understand. "Sure, Danny. I can help." He then warmed up the dinner that Meredith had left for him. As he ate, he made casual conversation with Lauren and the kids. After he rinsed out his dish, he walked over to where Danny and Sophie were using cookie cutters to cut out pieces of heart-shaped dough.

"Here, Mark," Danny said, handing him the cookie cutter. "You try."

"Okay," Mark said, rolling up his sleeves.

Lauren placed each cookie on the greased cookie sheet. They spent a half hour filling up three cookie sheets which Lauren put in the oven. Mark asked the kids how they had celebrated Valentine's Day at school while Lauren mixed up some powdered sugar icing. When she was done, Danny and Sophie both fought over who got to put the red food coloring into the icing. Lauren let each of them squeeze three drops and then mixed up the icing. As they waited for the cookies to cool, they all cleaned up the kitchen.

"Mark, when the cookies are done, we're gonna watch *Be My Valentine, Charlie Brown*. Wanna watch with us?"

"Danny, he might have plans. It is Valentine's Day, you know."

Mark chuckled. "If you're referring to a date, I don't have one."

Lauren smiled. "Well, if you would like to, we'd love your company watching Charlie Brown suffer through Valentine's Day, along with the rest of us single people."

"I love Charlie Brown," he responded.

When all the cookies had been iced, Lauren took a plate of them, along with two bowls of popcorn, into the downstairs family room. They all got comfortable on the couches and watched Charlie Brown strike out with the little red-haired girl.

By the time they finished watching it twice, it was time for bed. Both Danny and Sophie started complaining at the suggestion. It took a little coaxing, but they eventually agreed.

As Lauren went to walk them upstairs, she turned to Mark. "If you're not doing anything, we could watch a movie. Preferably nothing animated."

He grinned. "Yeah, okay. I'm not doing anything."

"Good. Well, I'll take these guys upstairs. Why don't you look through that console? There are a lot of movies, many of which I haven't seen yet. I buy movies, thinking they look good, but I never get time to watch them. Anyway, you pick out whatever you want. I'll be right back."

Lauren rushed through the bedtime routine, eager to join Mark in the family room. Was she being foolish? He didn't have anything better to do; it wasn't as if he'd ask her out on a date. After a bedtime story and a prayer, Lauren quickly brushed her hair and freshened up her face. When she got back down to the family room, Mark was seated on the couch, reading the back of a DVD.

"No, not that one," she said, walking toward him.

"Why not?" he asked, grinning up at her.

"I hate to watch my movies."

"Why?"

"Because I feel so self-conscious. You know, it's like hearing your voice on the answering machine."

"But I haven't seen this one," Mark said.

It was her fourth movie, based on the life of Sylvia Plath. "Please, not that one. There are, like, a hundred. Can't you find one that doesn't have me in it?"

He smiled stubbornly. "I don't want to see one of the others. Come on. I think I've only seen one of your movies. I really want to see it, please. Isn't it any good?"

"It is good, but I hate to watch myself on the screen. You're not going to insist on subjecting me to that, are you?"

He nodded. "Sorry, but I do insist."

Lauren rolled her eyes. "Okay, but just so you know, I'm not happy about this."

Mark smiled. "Oh, come on. Why don't you want me to watch it?"

Lauren moved over to the entertainment center and loaded the disc. "It's not so much that I don't want you to watch it. You can watch it. It's just that I don't want to watch it. I really hate seeing myself on screen."

Mark smiled at Lauren as she walked back to the couch. "Thank you."

She forced a smile. "You're welcome."

With Mark seated next to her, she felt more self-conscious than usual about watching her films. He would be watching her every move on screen.

Silence overtook the room as they watched Sylvia Plath's life unfold on film. Lauren was at least grateful he had picked a movie in which her performance had been praised. She was particularly proud of the film. Her eyes would occasionally turn to Mark, who was intently watching the movie. He asked sporadic questions about the film's location or a particular scene. Things turned a little uncomfortable for Lauren during a kissing scene. At least it wasn't one of her movies that had required extensive kissing or romance. It was a simple kiss between Sylvia and her husband, Ted, but Lauren was flooded with uncomfortable feelings as Mark intently watched the screen.

After the scene, he turned to her and smiled tentatively.

Lauren returned the smile, hers even more tentative.

He cleared his throat. "So, is that hard? Kissing someone for a movie?"

She shrugged. "It can be. It's not my favorite thing, but it's part of the art. It's just acting. Instead of reciting a line, it's an action. A kiss, but both of us knows it's a performance. We don't enjoy it or want it on a romantic level."

He nodded and continued watching. The movie neared its tragic end as the poet took her own life. As the ending credits rolled, Mark sighed. "That was really good. Sad, but good."

"I'm happy with the way it turned out."

He smiled. "You should be really proud. You're a wonderful actress."

Lauren had heard an excess of compliments throughout her career, but never had it warmed her heart, along with her cheeks as it did at that moment. Mark's one-sentence compliment made her blush, making it almost impossible to meet his eyes. "Thank you," was all she could say.

Mark looked at his watch. "Wow, it's late. I really appreciate you agreeing to let me watch the movie with you. I enjoyed it a lot," he said, standing up.

Lauren stood up and followed him toward the front door. "I'm glad you liked it."

"There are still several of your movies I haven't seen. Maybe someday you'll show them to me?"

"Maybe," she said warily.

As he reached the door, Mark turned around to face Lauren. "Well, Happy Valentine's Day," he said. "Have a good night."

"Good night," she said. "Do you mind giving us a ride to church tomorrow, since Tara's out of town?"

He smiled. "I'd love to. Anytime."

"Thank you," she said, closing the door behind him. She leaned her back against the door, her heart still pumping. Something in his eyes that night told her what she thought was impossible, was indeed possible.

The next day felt so right. As Mark drove them to church in his car, Lauren let herself, for just a moment, imagine what it would be like to be married to him, sitting beside him in the car. Could someone like Mark be able to see past the many years in which she had not lived the gospel? Would he be able to live with the sins she had committed? Lauren closed her eyes for a moment, trying to imagine it, but couldn't.

During sacrament meeting, Lauren felt the Spirit and the Savior's love strongly. She was being forgiven. She could rebuild her life, with his help, and come back to his fold. Throughout the meeting, she could feel the Spirit envelop her weary soul in love and acceptance. As the day continued, one lingering thought stayed in her mind. The Lord would accept her. There was no question about that. But could Mark ever accept her? Somehow, that seemed really important to her as she began to realize the extent of her feelings for him.

Lauren hated the thought of going to the premiere. She would much rather stay home with the kids, but her publicist had insisted. The film that was premiering, *To Each His Own,* starred Kevin Taylor, Lauren's costar in the film she was currently working on. Her attendance would show support for her costar, as well as give her an opportunity to be seen. Since her Oscar nomination had been announced, the film for which she was nominated began replaying in theaters. It didn't hurt to keep herself on people's minds. So, Lauren had agreed to attend. Thankfully, her good friend John Prentiss was in town doing a photo shoot and could accompany her.

She and John had been friends almost from the moment she had arrived in L.A. They had met at an audition and, after talking for a while, learned they had a lot in common. They were both the same age and struggling to make it in the business. Before long, they were sharing an apartment with four other starving actors.

Nothing romantic had ever occurred between the two of them. Somehow, they just both knew from the beginning that they were destined to be only friends. They had become very close friends and Lauren loved him like one of her brothers. Over the years, Lauren and John had looked out for each other. When Lauren had been particularly down on her luck, John had helped her out with rent or had given her money for food. And Lauren had helped John when he had struggled. They had bolstered each other when one's spirit had faltered. Lauren was quite sure that if it hadn't been for John's friendship and encouragement, she would have given up and gone home long before.

Of course, there were painful memories too. Lauren bit her lip and shut her eyes as she remembered the young, innocent man who became quickly tainted by the insidious offerings of a fast-paced life. John had instantly become friends with a crowd that coaxed him into trying substances that he'd never encountered before. Lauren had seen John disintegrate slowly amongst his new friends, who introduced him to a wild nightlife and the stimulating effects of drugs.

It was around that time that the two friends had started growing apart as each became increasingly involved in their own careers. Lauren remembered the first time she had seen John high. It had alarmed her greatly and she had talked to him, tried to convince him to never do it again, but it had only been the beginning. The numerous times she had spoken out against him using drugs had been pointless. He had continued throughout the years to use a variety of illegal and increasingly dangerous substances.

Eventually, John had given up on acting and turned to modeling, where he found his niche. He was taken in by a modeling agency and kept quite busy with photo shoots. Lauren landed her recurring role on the soap, *The Cutting Edge*.

After their careers took off, Lauren and John didn't spend as much time together but still managed to keep in touch. John began traveling, spending months at a time in New York City, and Lauren began to settle down in L.A.

Through the years, they managed to see each other when their schedules permitted. Lauren was extremely grateful for the opportunity to see him after more than a year. In town for only one day, it happened to coincide with the premiere she felt obligated to attend.

She slipped on the black Versace calf-length dress and strapped on a pair of black high-heeled sandals. After saying good night to Tara and the kids, she went downstairs and out to where Mark was waiting with the Mercedes. He greeted her and promptly opened the rear door. She entered the car and sat back.

A while later they parked outside the Beverly Hills Hotel, from which John emerged shortly. Dressed in a dark suit and bright red tie, he looked more handsome than ever. His dark hair was neatly trimmed. His bright blue eyes wore a hint of despair, as always. His smooth, clean-shaven face was as soft as a baby's skin. His tall, lean body was perfect for modeling. Despite his outwardly jovial self, Lauren knew John ached deep inside. No matter what level of success John obtained, it was never enough for him. He always wanted more and in no way felt he was good enough. He pushed himself to excel, and he had turned to drugs early on to assuage his feelings of inadequacy. Lauren had always refused to use any illegal substances—never even smoked a cigarette—and had hated to see John drown his hurt in the harmful substances. She hoped he was sober tonight.

Lauren stepped out of the car for a moment to greet him, throwing her arms around him and holding him in a warm embrace. "It's good to see you, Johnny."

"You too, Laurey. I've missed you."

They stepped into the car and Mark drove them to the Grauman's Chinese Theater, where the premiere was being held.

"You look good, Laurey. What have you done to yourself?"

"Nothing, really. Just taking better care of myself, I guess. How about you? You taking care of yourself?"

"Like always."

That's what Lauren was worried about. The way he took care of himself was not exactly what was best for him.

On the way toward Hollywood Boulevard, John and Lauren chatted about their current projects and ventures. Lauren was excited to hear John had landed a major contract for the top New York agency to represent him.

As they reached the Chinese Theater, they were led inside amidst photographers and reporters snapping pictures and throwing out questions as they walked past.

By the time the movie was over, a premiere party followed at the nearby Troupadour, a trendy Hollywood restaurant and nightclub. Lauren looked around at the familiar scene: nothing she hadn't seen before, something she was growing tired of. Beautiful faces created by Beverly Hills's best plastic surgeons. Starlets and leading men coupled with different dates than the last time. Glasses of Dom Perignon at your disposal. John quickly grabbed a glass of bubbly from the first proffered tray. Lauren declined and he gave her a curious look.

"I'm not drinking anymore."

John stopped walking. "Not drinking anymore? What do you mean?"

Lauren continued to walk, and he was forced to follow her.

"I'm giving up booze. I'm giving up a lot of things. I want to live my standards again. I'm really not sure why I ever stopped."

"You mean, you're doing the Mormon thing again?"

"Yes," she huffed. She didn't care for the way he termed it. "I want to be someone my kids can look up to and admire. Is that so strange?"

"They still look up to you even if you have a glass of Merlot," he said, handing her a glass of wine he'd just grabbed off one of the server's trays.

Lauren pushed the glass away. "No, none for me. I'm serious."

"You are serious, aren't you?" he said, drinking the wine in one easy gulp. He placed the empty glass on another server's tray as they continued further into the restaurant.

Lauren greeted several people she knew and introduced John to some of them. She'd grown tired of the same routine. This was starting to get old. The same people and the same inane conversation. The only thing that was different was the assortment of lavish and ridiculously priced outfits. She looked at her own dress and wondered if she honestly needed half the clothes she owned. She and John walked to the bar, where he ordered a Bloody Mary. She chose a club soda and used it to take an Advil she kept at the bottom of her purse.

John spotted a supermodel he recognized from a shoot he'd done several months before and excused himself to go talk to her. Lauren leaned against the bar and asked herself what she was doing here. None of this pleased her anymore.

"You're Lauren Olsen," said a voice from behind her.

She turned around to see a man she didn't recognize. Guessing he was probably around her age, she had to admit he was good-looking. A tall, trim, athletic body was enhanced by his tanned and rugged face and his dark hair. Ordinarily, she would have been immediately attracted to him, but she'd learned the hard way what charming and handsome men in Hollywood were really like.

She smiled politely. "I am Lauren Olsen."

He took her hand and squeezed it. "I'm Arthur Ramsey, Kevin's friend. We go way back from our days on *General Hospital*."

"It's nice to meet you," Lauren said, hoping John was coming back soon. From the looks of his intimate conversation with the supermodel, it wasn't likely.

Arthur looked in the direction of John and the model. "Is that your date?"

"He's my friend."

"So, he's not your date?"

"We are here together, but we're just friends."

Arthur smiled. "I've been wanting to meet you for some time now. I've been trying to get Kevin to introduce us, but he's so busy, and I guess he thought you were with someone."

Lauren groaned inwardly. Where was John? She turned to see he was completely oblivious to her situation. Turning back to Arthur, she forced a smile. "I'm not really with anyone at the moment, but it's actually a good thing. I've been able to spend more time with my kids. Did Kevin mention I have two children?" She hoped the idea of a single mother would turn him away in search of a different unattached Hollywood actress.

"Yes, I know that. I have two children as well. I don't get to see them as often as I'd like. They each live with their mothers."

Lauren drank the rest of her club soda and willed John to come save her from Arthur's clutches. She was becoming increasingly aware that he was the last man she wanted to be spending time with.

"Let me refill your drink," Arthur said, taking her glass. He held it up for inspection. "What were you drinking?"

"Club soda."

Arthur laughed. "I'll get you a martini. They have the best martinis here." He held up his hand to get the bartender's attention.

"No, thank you." Lauren grabbed his arm. "I don't want a martini."

Arthur eyed her curiously. "So, are you more of a champagne person?"

"No, I don't want a drink," she said to Arthur and the bartender simultaneously. Once the bartender had walked away, Lauren turned back to Arthur. "I don't drink."

Arthur nodded understandingly. "After my stint in rehab, I tried the sober thing too. It only lasted ten days." He shrugged. "I don't know how some people do it."

Lauren bit her lip, trying to hold back what she really wanted to say. "I didn't have a stint in rehab. I just don't drink."

"That's okay. I still like you," Arthur said, smiling.

Lauren turned to look for John and thankfully he was walking toward her. Grateful for her escape, she latched onto his arm. She introduced him to Arthur and the two men exchanged pleasantries.

"It was nice to meet you, Arthur," Lauren said. "Excuse me, but I've been wanting to catch Rudolph Williams and I see him right over there."

"Hopefully I'll see you around." He winked as she turned to walk away, pulling John behind her. She made her way toward a small table where the famed director, Rudolph Williams, sat. He was a rotund man who made his presence known through his booming voice and the cigar smoke that followed him everywhere. Despite the disgusting odor of the smoke that surrounded him, she wanted the chance to speak to him.

It was nearing midnight when Lauren called Mark on the cell phone to have him pick them up. She felt bad for keeping him out late, but it really didn't happen too often and it was Friday night, so at least he didn't have class the following day.

Lauren hadn't wanted to stay that late, but had gotten into a productive conversation with Rudolph Williams, a director she'd wanted to work with for a long time. They talked about some upcoming projects and planned to get together to do lunch later in the month. Mark was waiting for them as Lauren and John came out. He opened the door, and she thanked him as she followed John into the car.

"Kickin' party, Laurey," John said as he settled in.

"Yeah, not bad," Lauren said, thinking she would probably have enjoyed it a few months ago, but the Hollywood parties had lost much of their appeal.

"Arthur Ramsey was quite taken with you."

Lauren laughed. "No, thank you! I was just being nice because he's Kevin's friend. Kevin and I have to get along for at least the remainder of filming."

"Well, he was being more than a little nice to you."

"I'm not interested. I've sworn off men—at least his kind of men."

"I still can't believe you've gone back to being Mormon. You didn't even have one drink tonight."

"I told you, John, I don't drink anymore."

"And how long is that going to last?"

"Forever. I don't plan on ever drinking again."

"And no men like Arthur?"

"No!"

John shook his head. "Hard to believe."

Lauren laughed. "I don't care. I've turned over a new leaf—or an old leaf, I guess it would be. I'm back to living like I should have been all these years."

"As long as you're happy."

"I am," she said. "More than ever. And, while we're on the subject, John, you should think about giving up a few things in your life."

"Don't start with me, Laurey."

"John, you could be so happy if you'd just listen to what I have to say."

John shook his head. "That kind of life may be right for you, but not me, so drop it."

"Fine," she said, feeling that if he would just listen to the gospel, he could find the relief and comfort he had always sought in drugs. She felt ashamed as she realized that in thirteen years, this was the first time she'd tried to share the gospel with him. She hadn't been living it before, so how could she possibly share it? "So, you're leaving tomorrow?"

He nodded. "Yeah, back to New York."

"Are you excited about the new agency?"

"A whole new world. They're going to open doors for me—really skyrocket my career."

Lauren worried that this whole new world would put more pressure on John than he needed. She imagined that with his skyrocketing career would come more anxiety and perhaps also a higher level of drug usage. She knew John's usage increased with the demands that were placed on him. "Just be careful. I'm worried about you."

"Don't worry, Laurey. I can take care of myself."

Lauren sighed. She didn't want him taking care of himself—not in the manner he usually did.

John gave her a peck on the cheek and stepped out of the car, waving halfheartedly as he turned to walk toward the hotel. As he disappeared into his hotel, a new set of worries occurred to Lauren. What did Mark think of John? Did he think that he was an ex-boyfriend or a current love interest? John was like a brother to her, and Lauren wanted to be sure Mark knew that. Even though there was little hope of Mark being truly interested in her, she wanted him to know there was no one standing in the way.

She cleared her throat, trying to think of the right words. "He's just a friend. We've been friends for a long time." That didn't sound right—a little contrived and sort of out of nowhere.

Mark looked into the rearview mirror and caught Lauren's eye. "It's good to have friends."

"My best friend, sort of like a brother. He was there when I had no one else. When I first moved out here, I had no money, knew no one; he was pretty much in the same boat, and we kind of helped each other along. There were times I didn't have a cent and was too ashamed to ask my parents for help. He'd pay for my meals and my part of the rent and he never asked for the money back. He was like a brother. He was like the family I missed so much. I would never have made it if it weren't for him. I was close to giving up and going home so many times and he kept me going."

"Sounds like he's a pretty good friend."

"He is. We've never been romantically involved, though.

He has a new girlfriend almost every week, and I've never been one of them." Okay, she was rambling now, maybe even sounding a little idiotic, but she just wanted Mark to know for sure.

He looked up into the mirror again and smiled.

When Mark pulled up in front of the house, Lauren got out as he opened the door. "I'm sorry I kept you so late. Sleep in tomorrow. We probably won't go anywhere until the afternoon. I'm sure the kids will want to do something."

"Okay," he said, closing the door behind her.

"Thanks," she said, turning to go into the house. After taking one step, she turned around. "I just wanted you to know that John is only my friend. I know I already said that, but I just wanted to be sure you knew that."

"I'm glad you told me," Mark said.

Lauren nodded and hurried into the house before she made a bigger fool of herself. At least he knew.

Lauren sat in an overstuffed leather chair in her office reading one of the scripts that had arrived by messenger. Danny and Sophie were taking turns playing a game on the computer. Although they had a computer in the upstairs family room, they always enjoyed playing in her office. It was a special treat for them.

The phone rang, and Lauren stood to answer it. It was Rich.

"Hi, sis. How's everyone?"

"We're doing well. You?"

"Well, good, but I have some bad news."

"What?"

"I can't make it next week."

"Rich!"

"I'm sorry, but I got that new job, and they won't let me take the time off."

"Well, I'm glad about your job, but I really wanted you

to come to the Oscars with me."

"I really did too. Not just to go with you, but I'm dying to see Tara. It's only been a week, but I miss her. She's really going to be mad."

Lauren sighed. "She'll get over it and I will too, but we were both looking forward to seeing you. This job, is that important?"

"Yes! I mean, it's just a part-time job for the afternoons, but they're going to work with my class schedule."

"What will you be doing?"

"Technical support. I'm sorry. I really am."

"I know, Rich. Maybe Jacob would want to come."

"I already asked him. He wanted to go, but he has a mid-term Monday morning. He doesn't want to risk getting back late."

Lauren sighed. "It's okay. I'll find someone to go with me."

"I guess I'd better call Tara and break the news."

"I think she's in her room."

"Okay. I'll call her. Bye."

As Lauren hung up the phone, she sighed and slumped back down into her chair. What now? It was only a week away and she needed a date; she couldn't just show up by herself. Not able to concentrate on the script, she tossed it to the ground and sat back to think. An idea formulated in her mind.

"Hey, you guys. I'll be back in a few minutes." She went into the bathroom and brushed her hair, checked her makeup, and walked through the garage to the apartment upstairs.

She paused at Mark's door for a moment, having second thoughts, and then knocked before she could change her mind.

He answered the door and stepped back. "Hi."

"I hope I'm not interrupting. Can I talk to you for a minute?"

"Sure. Come in," he said, stepping away from the door.

Lauren entered, looking around the room. "I haven't been

up here in so long." Her eyes went directly to a desk with the framed picture of Danny that he'd given Mark for Christmas. "Kim used to live here before she got engaged."

"It's a really comfortable apartment. I appreciate you letting me stay here."

"Sure. I'm sorry that it's such a girl room. Kim picked out the couch and curtains. I guess you can tell she likes flowers. If you don't like it, we can order some new furniture. Something a little more masculine."

He shook his head and laughed. "That's okay. I probably won't be staying that much longer."

"Right," she said, remembering he would be graduating soon and off to start a new life, away from her. She almost couldn't bear the thought. "Again, I'm sorry to barge in on you, but I wanted to ask you a favor."

"Sure."

Lauren hesitated and then cleared her throat. "It's a personal favor, you know. It doesn't have anything to do with work."

"Okay."

"I have an awards show to go to on the twenty-seventh and, well, Rich was going to fly in to go with me, but he started a new job and, well, they won't give him the time off, so I'm sort of left without a date. You don't have to say yes, you know, don't feel obligated just because you work for me, but if you are free that day, I would appreciate it."

"I'll ask my boss to see if I can get the time off."

Lauren laughed. "I think she probably would give you the night off. Maybe she'll hire a limo service that night."

Mark smiled. "I'd love to go with you, Lauren."

She smiled, meeting his eyes for a second, and then looked away. "Well, thank you. If it's okay with you, the people from Hugo Boss are coming this week for a fitting."

"A fitting?"

"For your tux."

"Can't I just rent a tuxedo?"

Lauren laughed. "No, sorry. Um, you can't really wear a rented tux. Besides, I've had calls from so many people wanting to outfit my date and I decided to go with Hugo Boss. It's complimentary. All you have to do is make sure everyone knows who you're wearing."

Mark chuckled. "Okay. Well, it's not like it's the Oscars or anything."

Lauren laughed. "Well, actually it is."

"You're inviting me to the Oscars?"

She nodded. "Is that okay?"

"Yeah, I just didn't know it was the Oscars. You just said it was an award show."

"I know. I just didn't want you to feel overwhelmed by it."

"No, I'm just flattered."

She smiled. "I wanted to ask you because, well, most of my friends in the business don't understand the standards I'm trying to live by now. I wanted to share the night with someone who believes the same as I do, someone who wouldn't be drinking or wouldn't expect anything at the end of the night."

He smiled. "I'm really honored that you would ask me. I can't think of anything I'd rather do than go to the Oscars with you."

The next week passed quickly as Lauren anticipated Oscar night. She had been to the Academy Awards before, but never as a nominee. The days were kept busy at the set, and afternoons and evenings were filled with preparations such as press releases, phone interviews, and looking through dresses that various designers had sent over in hopes that Lauren would wear one.

Mark and Lauren seemed to enjoy a happy camaraderie as they awaited the arrival of Oscar night. He was very gracious about the numerous fittings for his Hugo Boss tuxedo. Lauren had Kim make arrangements for the limo service, hairdresser, makeup, and manicurist. It seemed like the day would never arrive, but it finally did.

Lauren spent most of the day getting ready. A masseuse came in for an extended session to get Lauren relaxed for the big night. An endless line of hair and makeup people also came to the house to help Lauren prepare. Kim had done an excellent job in arranging for every minute detail and Lauren was grateful that her personal assistant knew when to step up.

Mark straightened his shirt and struggled to tie his bowtie. He couldn't remember the last time he'd worn a tuxedo—probably at his brother's wedding. He tugged a few more times on his bow tie and walked over to the mirror above his dresser. It seemed all right. As he pulled on the tuxedo jacket, he wondered what the big deal was about Hugo Boss. It looked like an ordinary tuxedo, nothing special—just like anything he could have rented.

He passed a comb through his still-damp hair. Shaking his head, he said to himself, "I can't believe I'm going to the Oscars."

Walking toward the living room, he picked up a small bouquet of pink tulips he had bought for Lauren. Mark felt unusually nervous about this date. Was it because it was such a huge event or because of the woman he was going with? He wasn't sure. The thought of going on a date with Lauren made his pulse race. Mark wasn't sure when he had first realized his feelings for her. He couldn't exactly explain what those feelings were, but there was definitely an attraction, a connection that made him like being with her. Did she feel the same way too? He was almost certain she did, but she had only asked him on this date because Rich couldn't make it.

Mark wiped his palms on his pants, hoping that Hugo Boss wouldn't mind. He went down the stairs and decided to ring the doorbell to make things more formal. Kim answered the door.

"Hi, handsome," she said, moving aside to let him in. "I see Hugo Boss lived up to his reputation."

"Thanks," Mark said as he walked into the foyer.

"Lauren will be down in a few minutes," Kim said and then explained the limo drop-off and red carpet routines. "Here are some sunglasses that the Versace people sent over. Put them on as soon as you get out of the limo. You make sure to get out first and then help her out. Lauren will be greeted by throngs of fans and media. She'll have to acknowledge them. You just ignore them and help usher her toward the entrance, but don't come off as a snob, just sort of nonchalant. Don't be nervous. You're not nervous, are you? You can't seem nervous. Just play it cool. Whatever you do, don't seem overwhelmed by the other actors. Nicholson will be there, so will Eastwood and Roberts and anyone who's anyone, but you can't seem the least bit fazed by it. And you can't ask for an autograph. You weren't going to, right? No, of course not. You have to act like you've been there before, like you belong. They're going to ask about your relationship. Don't answer anything specific. Just be vague. Don't give them any information they can use against you. When they stop you guys to interview Lauren, don't look around. You can't be distracted by who's walking around you. You keep your eyes on Lauren. Who cares about anyone else? She's the star. Got it?"

"I think so," Mark said, wondering how she managed to breathe when she just went on and on.

"The post-Oscars parties. You'll have to go to *Vanity Fair's*, at least. Don't go up to anyone. Let them approach you. You're with Lauren Olsen. She's a star. There will be interviews at every stop, whether she wins or not. Hopefully she'll win," Kim said, crossing her fingers. "If she doesn't, she can't seem too disappointed. I already told her that, you have to remind her. She just waves it off, like it's not a big deal, right? You'll do fine. You're not nervous, right? Remember, play it cool. Nonchalant. Don't notice anyone. You're with Lauren Olsen, who cares about anyone else."

As they talked, Danny and Sophie came bounding down the stairs, interrupting whatever instruction Kim was going to give next.

"She's coming," Tara said, following behind them.

Mark watched as Lauren descended the stairs. Her beauty coupled with her graceful movements caught him off guard. Dressed in a black, silky formfitting gown, she'd never looked so beautiful.

He couldn't take his eyes off her. As she came down the stairs, Lauren focused on her feet, pulling up the length of her dress as she took each step. When she reached the last step, she looked up, finally meeting his eyes. She smiled, noting his complete admiration.

Mark walked toward her, holding out the small bouquet, which now seemed trite in the grandeur of her beauty. "You look wonderful."

"Thank you," Lauren said, taking the bouquet. "You don't look so bad yourself."

Kim, Tara, and the kids took turns telling Lauren how beautiful she looked. Kim picked up a camera from a small table near the stairs. She directed Mark and Lauren to stand together as she took several shots. Then Kim took a few pictures of Mark and Lauren with the kids.

After nearly a dozen pictures, Lauren turned to Mark. "Get used to it. It'll be worse than this when we get there."

Mark chuckled.

"Okay, Kim. That's enough. You act like it's the prom or something."

"One more, one more," Kim said, holding out her hand in an attempt to keep them from moving. "Put your arm around her, Mark. Okay, both of you smile. Say, 'Oscar.' Wait, just one more."

Mark obliged, wondering if Lauren was uncomfortable with the gesture. Tara took the bouquet from Lauren, saying she would put them in a vase.

Kim came over to where they were standing to coach Lauren on her interview etiquette. "Remember, Carolina Herrera dress, Harry Winston necklace, Mark Jacobs shoes, and Versace bag. You can't forget. They want their plugs. Whatever you do, avoid Joan Rivers. Try to steer in her daughter's direction. Melissa is so much nicer at interviewing. The last thing you want is Joan Rivers saying something about your high neckline. Plunging necklines are in this year. She's been saying that for months. I'm still not sure about your neckline. Are you sure, Lauren? We still have the low-cut Donna Karan upstairs. We can get you into that. You'll definitely have the least revealing dress. Everyone else is going to be showing skin. We should have at least gone with the backless dress—or the strapless. Are you sure? Never mind, you already decided. Sorry. The dress looks great. Just don't run into Joan."

Lauren sighed. "We should get going," she said. Mark put his hand on the small of her back and steered her toward the door. The others followed close behind. Lauren turned around to face Danny and Sophie before she approached the car. "You guys be good. You can stay up late tonight because my category is toward the end. Keep your fingers crossed for me," she said, hugging Danny. "I love you," she said as she hugged Sophie. Lauren waved good-bye to Kim and Tara, and then Mark walked her to the open limo door. He followed her inside and then leaned back against the plush, leather interior.

"How do you feel?" he asked.

"Like Cinderella. Charming prince and all."

He laughed. "I don't know about that."

"Thank you so much for coming with me."

"I have to say I am excited. I've never been to anything like this before."

When she smiled again, Mark felt a fluttering inside his stomach. Was it just the pure magic of the evening that caused the stirring inside? As he took a long look at Lauren, he knew it was more than that. She was what was affecting him so much. He had tried for weeks to push aside his growing feelings for her. But tonight as he sat beside her in the luxury of the limo on the way to the Oscars, he couldn't deny what he was feeling toward her. The emotion had been threatening to emerge for weeks, and finally it had come full throttle the moment he saw her descending the stairs.

Despite the roominess of the limo, Mark was seated right beside her, his leg touching hers slightly. Was she feeling it too? Silence pervaded the limo for several moments as they watched each other. She smiled and Mark felt it again. He returned her smile and reached out to gently stroke her cheek with his fingertips.

"You're so beautiful," he said, allowing his fingers to linger on her face, feeling its softness, indulging in its beauty.

Her smile broadened and Mark thought he detected a subtle coloring in her cheeks.

"You probably hear that a lot," he said, finally pulling his hand away from her face.

"Maybe, but it's never sounded more sincere or been more appreciated than right now. Hearing you say it means so much to me. You couldn't possibly understand."

"I think I do," he said. In her line of work, where beauty was so important and Lauren was a purveyor of it, she was probably showered with compliments on a daily basis. Perhaps hearing it meant more coming from someone outside of the business, someone who didn't have to say it but wanted to.

The tense moment dissipated as Lauren told Mark what to expect. Kim had already told him most of it, but he didn't mind hearing it again. The entire phenomenon was so new to him that a repetition of what to expect was welcomed. "Every guy with a mike will want five minutes with me. I have to stop and talk to them, answer the same inane questions. Whose dress am I wearing? Who lent me the jewelry? What did I do today to prepare myself? Am I nervous? And after taking one look at you, I'm sure everyone will be asking who my handsome date is."

Mark laughed and shook his head.

"Actually, it's going to be pretty boring for you and I apologize. While I'm being interviewed, you won't have much to do, but I'll try to get through it as fast as I can. We're a little behind schedule, which is a good thing. I'll be one of the last ones to arrive, so hopefully, they'll rush me through. Everyone will be anxious to get inside."

Mark asked her a few questions about the process and they spoke a little more about the evening. Before he knew it, they had arrived at the Kodak Theater on Hollywood Boulevard. It was an overwhelming sight as he looked out the window. The limo waited for its turn to pull over and Mark took in all that lay before him. To his left were swarms of fans and onlookers across the street, held back by a barricade and an army of police officers. To his right, amongst the flashes of countless cameras were throngs of people dressed in shimmering gowns and dark suits. Television cameras abounded and it seemed a person couldn't get through without running into a reporter or photographer of some kind.

As their limo reached the point of entrance, their door was opened and Mark exited and helped Lauren out. Immediately, a smile covered her face and she began waving to the crowds across the street as they shouted her name. She took a few moments to wave and then they continued toward the building.

Lauren had warned him, but Mark was still not prepared for the onslaught of people that approached them. Reporter after reporter stopped them and raved over her dress, her hair, everything. Each stop replicated itself as the same questions were asked, the same exuberant compliments given, and the same good luck wished. Mark mostly stood on the sidelines as Lauren faced the "inane questions," as she had termed them. He was grateful to not be included in the interviews and was mostly ignored with the attention focused on Lauren. Instead, he stood back, fading into the background, obscured by the dark glasses Kim had given him. A few times, he was included in an interview because a few reporters were curious about who Lauren Olsen's date was. Lauren introduced him as a good friend and Mark mostly smiled or commented on how wonderful Lauren looked. He was thankful when the red carpet process was over. Once inside, away from the cameras and screaming fans, he felt more at ease.

His ease was short-lived and a sense of awe overcame it as he walked further into the immense Kodak Theater. Images of famous Oscar winners were displayed as photographic transparencies on clear Plexiglas hung in front of shimmering beaded panels. The wall-sized lobby windows offered a panoramic view of the Hollywood hills. They then walked down hallways studded with shimmering beads.

As they walked into the main theater, Mark felt as though he was walking into an old opera house with balconies on either side. The balconies were decorated in rich blue and wine fabric with glass material on the front that seemed to glow.

Mark took Lauren's hand as they were led down the long corridor toward their assigned seats two rows back from the stage. He held on to her hand as they sat down.

She sighed. "We made it. Thanks for your patience through all that garbage."

He smiled and squeezed her hand. "It wasn't bad. I can't believe some of the people I saw. This is quite the star-studded event."

She laughed. "Yeah, it is."

Mark looked up toward the cathedral-like ceiling, noticing the intricate decor. A sort of tiara was intertwined with smaller ovals, coated in silver leaf. The entire theater was amazing. He surveyed the people sitting directly around them, disbelieving that he was sitting among so many famous people. As Kim had emphasized, he tried to be nonchalant, but it was almost impossible because he was seated right across the aisle from Clint Eastwood. He reached over and took Lauren's hand. "Are you nervous?"

"I just wish the Best Actress category wasn't toward the end. I want to get it over with. I don't know if I can sit through this whole ceremony."

He leaned over and whispered in her ear. "You'll do fine. I'm sure of it. If you start to get nervous, just squeeze my hand."

She smiled. "Okay."

The orchestra began playing, and the ceremony commenced. The host, a well-known comedian, entertained the crowd for a full twenty minutes before introducing the first presenters. The ceremony seemed to drag a little at times, but for the most part Mark enjoyed it. Lauren seemed to relax as one award was presented after another. They exchanged remarks during some parts of the ceremony. Mark asked her a few questions about one actor or another, and he enjoyed her insight on several of the presenters.

By the time most of the awards had been presented, the ceremony was running behind schedule. The previous year's Best Actor winner was introduced to present the Best Actress award.

Lauren shifted in her chair and then reached for Mark's hand. He felt her grip tighten as they began to announce the nominees. She quickly flashed a smile, not indicative of the anxiety Mark felt quite certain she was feeling. Lauren smiled into the camera as they read her name, along with the names of the other women nominated for Best Actress.

As the presenter opened the envelope, Mark's pulse quickened, in nervousness and anticipation for Lauren. Her feeling seemed to echo his own as she squeezed his hand more tightly, almost bracing herself for the announcement.

"And the Oscar goes to . . . Lauren Olsen."

Lauren gasped, putting her hand to her mouth as she stood up. A hearty applause followed as Mark stood up with Lauren and helped steady her by taking her arm. She turned to him and he kissed her cheek, releasing her arm as she walked into the aisle and up the few steps to the microphone. Vague memories of tabloid covers stirred in his mind as he released her. For some reason, it didn't seem to matter tonight. A sense of magic seemed to dispel any worries about tomorrow's magazine covers.

Mark sat down, feeling his heart beating fast. She won! He wasn't sure why he was so happy for her, but he was. As he watched her on the center stage, he wondered how he could feel so tied to her. He had felt her victory so strongly, almost as if it had been his own.

Lauren clutched the Oscar as she leaned into the microphone. "Thank you so much. I know every nominee secretly hopes to win, but is never foolish enough to believe they will. I know I didn't believe I could win. I am so grateful for this honor. I need to thank Marty Woods, my agent, who fought to get me this part. Kenton Davies, the best director to work for, all the people at Styson Pictures, Kelson Thomie, Bruce Simonson, thank you for the wonderful opportunity to work for you. To the entire cast and crew, it was an amazing experience. Thank you to my manager, Sol, to Kim, and to Tara. Danny and Sophie, thank you for being the best kids a mom could ask for. I love you. Thank you to my entire family for undying love despite everything. Mark, thanks for coming with me tonight. Your friendship means more to me than you will ever know. Thank you to the Academy for a great honor. Good night." Lauren waved to the crowd as she walked offstage.

The beauty and grace with which Lauren accepted the

Oscar award moved him. It took a while before Lauren returned to her seat. In a few moments, they would announce the final award of the night—best movie. Mark leaned over to whisper in Lauren's ear. "Congratulations. You looked beautiful up there."

"Thanks," she said, clutching the small statue toward her chest.

"How do you feel?"

"Amazing," she said. "I can't even describe it. I'm overwhelmed, exuberant, happy." She sighed. "I can't believe I won."

"I can," he said, fingering the smooth texture of the gold Oscar. His fingers moved from the Oscar to Lauren's hand. He caressed her fingers and leaned over to kiss the side of her face. "I'm really happy you won."

"Thank you," she said, taking his hand. She smiled at him, holding his gaze. For a moment they looked deep into each other's soul, oblivious to the excitement around the Best Picture Oscar being awarded. Mark didn't hear which movie won and didn't really care. All that mattered was the woman in front of him and how she made him feel.

The moment was broken as the ceremony ended and the theater began to clear out. Mark took Lauren's hand and led her out as he followed the crowd in front of him. Lauren went into the pressroom, where she stood before dozens of reporters who asked her questions regarding her win. When she finally made her way out of the pressroom, Lauren and Mark were taken back to the limo. Once inside, Lauren's excitement continued as her cell phone rang with congratulatory calls from her family, Kim, Tara and the kids, as well as her agent and manager. Mark was barely able to say a word as the phone rang without interruption. After finishing with Danny and Sophie, she urged them to go to sleep and told them she loved them. "Everyone's excited," she said, hanging up the phone.

Mark smiled. "I bet. Can I see it?"

As Lauren handed him the Oscar, he ran his fingers along the writing and studied the heavy object. "It's incredible."

"I know," she said. "Listen, we don't have to stay out too late, but I should at least show up to the *Vanity Fair* party, and then we can go home."

Mark shook his head as he handed her back the Oscar. "No way. We have to celebrate. This is a big night for you, and we are going to stay out all night, hit every big party."

Lauren laughed. "We don't really have to, if you don't want."

"Are you kidding? This is a once-in-a-lifetime thing. It's not every day you win an Oscar. We have to celebrate."

"Okay," she said. "Only if you're sure."

"Positive," he said. He took her hand and held it to his lips.

They spent the next few hours going from one party to the next. At every stop, they were once again bombarded with the media wanting to ask Lauren questions about her Oscar win. Mark was stunned by all the famous faces he saw. Lauren introduced him to many people as they came over to congratulate her. It felt strange to be among so many people who were sipping champagne as he and Lauren drank their Sprites. Despite the unfamiliar surroundings, Mark enjoyed himself. Lauren held onto his arm for most of the night as they moved around, mingling and greeting different people she knew. Mark was surprised that he had several good conversations with men he had only seen before on the big screen. Most of the people they talked to seemed warm and friendly and genuinely happy for Lauren's win. It was vastly different from what he had expected; it was actually enjoyable.

It was nearly two in the morning when he and Lauren turned to each other with the same expression, which seemed to say it was time to go home. The limo met them outside and Mark climbed in after Lauren, finally starting to feel the effect of exhaustion setting in. He sighed as he slid closer to Lauren, almost instinctively putting his arm around her. In a likewise instinctive manner, Lauren scooted next to him, resting her head on his shoulder.

The limo started off, and Mark closed his eyes, taking in all that he experienced. Lauren was quiet as she made herself comfortable against his shoulder. Mark turned toward Lauren and kissed the top of her head, breathing in the sweet smell she emanated. He pulled back slightly and touched her chin with his fingertips, gently raising her head toward his. "I had a wonderful time, Lauren. Thanks for inviting me to be your date. That's the best date I've ever had."

She smiled, looking deeply into his eyes. "Really?"

Mark nodded, his fingers still gingerly lifting her chin. "You looked so beautiful tonight. That dress, your hair, your face. You were the most beautiful woman in the whole place." With her face so close to his, how could he not do what his heart longed to do? He leaned in closer and pressed his lips to hers. He kissed her softly and she responded immediately.

13

The next morning, Mark awoke and willed himself to get out of bed, but it didn't come easily. After several minutes of deep thought, he forced himself to get up. A long shower finally made him alert, more alert than he'd really intended. He thought about last night, more specifically about kissing Lauren. It had seemed that she was just as enthralled by their kiss as she had been.

What exactly was she feeling? Had she just been overwhelmed by winning the Oscar? She had said she felt like Cinderella. Was her response to the kiss just the perfect ending to the fairy-tale night or was there more to it than that? Had she just kissed him because she believed that was expected of her at the end of the date? Or had she felt the same deepening attraction toward him that he'd been feeling for weeks? Was last night a culmination of their growing friendship and unde-niable attraction? Did she feel it too? Would their kiss lead to something?

All of these questions danced through his mind as the longing to see, hold, and kiss her again set in. He got dressed, hoping to see Lauren before she left for the onslaught of inter-views she had scheduled. Charlie was driving her to Burbank for a host of different appointments she had to discuss winning the Oscar.

As he was about to walk out of the apartment, his hand on the doorknob about to open the door to a whole new world, he paused. Slowly, he let go of the doorknob, walked away from the door and sat down on the couch with a loud sigh.

What was he thinking? He couldn't do it. He couldn't step into Lauren's world and become a part of it. The life she led was completely different from the way he intended to live his. Minutes from now she would be on nationwide television being interviewed for receiving an Academy Award. Her life was filled with limos and movie stars. He was a simple law student who led a simple life. She had more money than he would ever see in ten lifetimes. How could they possibly make a relationship work? Especially one centered on the gospel. As he looked out the window, he saw Lauren step into the Mer-cedes and Charlie drove her away. He wanted to run out to her and take her into his arms, but his body wouldn't move. It was almost as if he knew it was doomed if he tried to pursue anything with Lauren.

Mark rubbed his forehead, trying to force his mind to focus. He cared for Lauren. She was generous and kind. It was evident that she loved her children and had raised them to be respectful, loving children he would be proud to call his own. Ideally, Lauren was a woman with whom he would love to spend eternity. She was loving, hardworking, outgoing, and loyal. And recently she'd made so many positive changes. She was vastly different from the woman he'd met that first night.

She dressed more modestly, had given up drinking and party-ing, went to church regularly, and from what he could see, was living a moral life. It was clear that she had a true desire to return to the righteousness of her youth, but her past was still there. It lingered over him like a black cloud, darkening the present, threatening to bring forth torrents of pain and misery. Could he live his life knowing what Lauren's life had been like? He didn't know the extent of her indiscretions, but he knew there were some. Could he get past those? Could he be with a woman who had been with other men? Had he kept himself worthy his entire life to share a wedding night with a woman who had not done the same for him?

Mark shook his head. It was too much to overcome, and it would never work. As much as he longed to be with Lauren, it didn't seem possible. The depressing thought stayed with him throughout the day as he dragged himself through classes. The battling thoughts in his mind coupled with the lack of sleep left him with little ability to concentrate. He was thankful when his final class was over and he was able to catch an hour's nap before having to pick Lauren up from the Burbank studio where she had spent the day in interviews.

His mind still swayed back and forth between hoping they could make a relationship work and the idea that it could never work out. He still wasn't sure what he wanted when he saw Lauren emerge from the building. His first instinct was to take her in his arms and kiss her as he'd done the night before, but the doubts still lingered. It wouldn't be fair to be aloof and distant, especially after he'd initiated the kiss last night. Mark just decided to leave things up in the air until he could gauge her reaction.

That wasn't easy to do as she approached the car with a smile. "Hi, Mark," she said.

"Hey, how'd it go?" he asked, desperately wanting to put his arms around her.

"Pretty good. I'm exhausted, though. I bet you are too," she said, getting into the front seat.

He took his seat behind the wheel, grateful that she spoke up.

"Uh, Mark. I think we should clear the air a little."

He nodded for her to go on.

She cleared her throat and then stared straight ahead, out the window. "About last night . . ."

"Yeah, I've been thinking about that too."

Lauren turned to face him. "It was a great night. Maybe we just got caught up in the magic of it all, you know. I mean, we were both dressed up, feeling pretty good. To my complete amazement, I won. The night was perfect and then you kissed me, and it became even more perfect." She paused and looked away for a moment. Mark didn't want to interrupt her train of thought. "I'm not sorry that you kissed me. It was amazing, to say the least, but I don't want you to feel like you owe me anything. I mean—," she said, turning her eyes away from him.

He touched her hand. "Go on. I promise I won't be upset with whatever you have to say."

"I just don't want you to feel pressure to pursue anything with me if you're not comfortable with it. I mean, we got caught up in the moment. You kissed me. If you want it to end there, I'll understand. If you don't feel like anything more could come out of it, it's okay. I don't want you to think that just because you kissed me last night, you have to do it again—not if you don't want to. I'm not going to hold you to anything, Mark. It's okay if you want to still just be friends."

Mark kept his eyes locked on Lauren's. Did she really mean it? Is that how she felt?

No, she was just giving him an out, letting him know she understood his confusion. It was as though she had crept into his mind and read his thoughts, saw his doubts, and answered his dilemma. He watched her for a moment, realizing that she hung on his every thought and word. It seemed like she hoped he would say it didn't matter, he wanted to be with her. She was leaving it up to him; the ball was in his court. Lauren wouldn't expect anything to come out of last night's kiss.

She wouldn't hold him to anything, so it was easy to decide. She had left the door wide open for him to take the coward's way out.

"You're probably right," he said with as gentle a smile as he could muster. He didn't miss the look of abject disappointment on her face as he continued. "We did get caught up in the moment and you looked so beautiful, but it is probably best that we just stay friends."

She nodded, almost too agreeably. "Yeah, friends is best."

He squeezed her hand. He could tell that was not what she wanted to hear; she had just given him the opportunity to back out of the possibility of a relationship without hurting either of them. "I'm glad we talked about this," he said, feeling that she probably wasn't, but it was all for the best.

The drive home was uncomfortable. Mark asked Lauren questions about her interviews and how it went. She answered his questions, elaborated on some, but it was clear that she was dejected and disappointed, and he had caused it.

★ ★ ★

At home, Lauren thanked Mark for picking her up and went into the house. Her mind wasn't on dinner, or even on the Disney movie she watched with Sophie and Danny. She was grateful when bedtime approached and she was left alone with her thoughts. Physical exhaustion, along with mental anguish over her conversation with Mark, forced her to the bed where she lay down. She clutched a throw pillow to her heart as she let the tears stream down. Lauren knew she didn't have a right to be angry; she was the one who suggested they just be friends. What was she expecting? A declaration of undying love? Perhaps she wasn't expecting one, but she was hoping for it.

Lauren had not wanted him to feel pressured into pursuing a relationship that perhaps he didn't want or wasn't ready for, so she'd left it up to him to accept her "let's be friends" idea or to say something in objection. He had chosen the former option—to be friends. If he had wanted more, he could have easily said so, but he hadn't. Mark had made it clear; they should just stay friends. He had been caught up in the moment last night when he kissed her and now nothing would come of it. That was, perhaps, what hurt the most.

For one brief moment, she had tasted of the splendor it was to be with Mark Ellege. She had allowed the deep recesses of her mind to entertain the possibility that someone like Mark could truly care for her. To have that image in her mind for just a short time and then have it taken away in the blink of an eye was more than she could bear. Enduring the fact that someone like Mark would never love her had been difficult but bearable. But after his kiss and the delectable instant in which she believed it could be, it was too much to have it vanish. It had been too foolish to believe Mark would ever love her. Disappointment and anguish were not strong enough to describe how she was feeling. As she tried to imagine how she would ever cope with seeing Mark again, she drifted off to sleep.

The next day Lauren was not looking forward to seeing Mark again. When he picked her up from the set, the look of aloofness on his face added to the uneasiness she had already been feeling. Conversation was minimal, and only basic and necessary words were exchanged. How had it come to this after the blissful night they had shared at the Academy Awards?

The duration of the week was as difficult and trying as their first exchange after the Oscars. She could tell Mark was also struggling with how to act around her. It really hurt her that the natural friendliness they'd shared was suddenly gone.

Lauren was overwhelmed by the amount of scripts being sent to her agent. After winning the Oscar, directors and producers were eager to get her signed for new projects. Thankfully, Marty had combed through the majority of them and had only forwarded her ones that he thought were worth reading. She had spent several nights that week reading over the scripts after Danny and Sophie went to bed.

She was finishing up one that director Rudolph Williams had sent over. Lauren was quite impressed with some of his previous projects and had been eager to work with him for years. She was grateful that she had finally been able to talk to him at the premiere she and John had attended several months before. But as she read through Rudolph's current script, she felt no desire to even consider the part. As she neared the final page, her cell phone rang. It was Marty, who wondered if she had finished the script.

"Rudy's really eager to meet with you, Lauren. Can I set something up for next week?"

Lauren hesitated. "I don't know. I think I'm going to pass on this one."

"What? Any of his scripts are almost guaranteed to gross big time, and it practically has Oscar written all over it."

"Marty, every page is filled with profanity. He has me saying something vulgar in almost every scene. I'm not doing it."

"Since when has that even mattered to you?"

"Since now. I'm not doing it. It's filth. I don't care if it's going to make big bucks. I don't even care if it guarantees me a nomination or even an Oscar."

"Lauren, this is not a wise decision. He wants you. You're going to just turn him down?"

Marty worked for her; why did he think he could try to change her mind? "I just won an Oscar. I think I've earned the right to turn down any project I don't feel good about."

"Why don't I set up a meeting in a couple of weeks? You could talk to Rudy about what you don't feel comfortable with. He's a reasonable man. I'm sure he's willing to hear what you have to say. He's probably even willing to take out some of the profanity. What do you say?"

"I don't know."

"Let me make the call. Just have lunch with him to discuss it. I'll tell him you're undecided."

Lauren still felt hesitant to be involved in a project she was sure would garner an R rating. Against her better judgment, she agreed to Marty's request for a lunch meeting with Rudolph.

14

Danny and Sophie had a week off for spring break. Lauren was grateful Gus had given her three days off, but the remaining two days were mandatory. The cast and crew were being flown out to Catalina Island to film several scenes on location. Lauren was thankful the helicopter would take them out in the morning and back home in the evening. Tara also had the week off of school for spring break, so she would be with Danny and Sophie on Thursday. The only glitch was that Tara was flying to Idaho on Friday for her sister's wedding. She would only be gone for the weekend, but with Tara gone on Friday, and Lauren in Catalina, Lauren had to ask Meredith to stay later to be with the kids. On occasion, Lauren turned to her willing housekeeper to watch the kids, but she didn't like to impose too much on Meredith. She already did so much in keeping the house clean and making wonderful meals. But Meredith also loved Danny and Sophie. Lauren trusted her implicitly and felt confident in leaving the children with her for one day.

As Thursday finally came to an end, Lauren was happy that the week was almost over. It had been an exhausting and eventful week. On Monday, she had taken the kids to the beach. Tuesday, they had gone to Disneyland. On Wednesday, she had taken them shopping and then spent the rest of the day at home, playing games with them. Today had been exhausting, filming all day at the Marina on Catalina. Gus, the director, had pushed them hard to try to finish the scenes in the two days they had scheduled. Lauren realized that taking it easy on them would only have meant possibly adding a third day to their already grueling schedule, which nobody wanted. Nevertheless, Lauren felt weary that evening as she climbed into the waiting Mercedes.

During the past week, conversation with Mark had seemed strained. When she looked at Mark, all she could see was him kissing her. She couldn't look at him and not want it to happen all over again. But they hadn't so much as talked about that night since their first discussion of it. Their failure to even mention it almost made it seem like it had never happened at all. Mark's stark aloofness had Lauren wondering, at times, if she had imagined the whole thing. Even so, during quiet times when she was all alone, she allowed her mind to visit that special night, an intimate moment she wished more than anything she could recapture. At those times, she closed her eyes and for only an instant was able to invoke that wondrous feeling of his lips against hers.

At that moment, with Mark at her side, driving her home, she shut all such thoughts out of her mind. They exchanged casual conversation on the drive home. A few cell phone calls interrupted the trite conversation, for which Lauren was thankful. However, when Meredith called, a wrench was thrown into Lauren's plans for an easy end to the week.

Meredith's son had broken his arm during a basketball game and would be having surgery. There was no way she could make it the next day to stay with Danny and Sophie. Lauren assured her not to worry. Meredith's son was her priority, and Lauren told Meredith that she needed to be with him. Meredith was distraught over letting Lauren down but also seemed anxious about her son's condition. Once again, Lauren insisted that she not worry about anything, but her son. Lauren understood what it was like to have a sick child and didn't want Meredith to occupy her thoughts with anything else.

Lauren wished Meredith the best and then hung up. She sighed, wondering what she would do. Tara was out of town and she couldn't even consider not going to work. Her presence was absolutely necessary in Catalina; she couldn't let down the entire cast and crew by not showing up.

"What's the matter?" Mark asked, interrupting her thoughts.

"Oh, Meredith's son broke his arm."

"I hope he's okay."

"Me too," Lauren said. "I'm left with a bit of a problem, though. She was going to watch Danny and Sophie for me tomorrow since Tara's out of town. Now I'm not sure what to do. Maybe I could call someone from church. Who do you think I could call?"

"Well, there are a few people I can think of, but what would you say about me watching them?"

"Oh, I couldn't ask you to do that."

"I don't have any classes. I'm on spring break too, so I'd be happy to."

"Well, I'm sure you have things to do."

"Not really," he said. "Please let me do this for you. I can keep the kids busy. We'll wash the car. Maybe I'll take them to a movie or something."

"Are you sure?"

Mark smiled. "Yeah, I'm sure."

"I wish I didn't have to work, but they're flying us out to Catalina again and I can't miss it."

"Don't worry about it, Lauren. I'm happy to do it."

"Well, I'll pay you."

Mark laughed. "No you won't. Would you have paid one of the sisters in the ward?"

"Of course," Lauren said in all seriousness.

"Lauren, you're missing the whole point. We're here to help each other out. I'm your friend. Friends do favors for each other, and you don't have to pay them for that."

Lauren smiled. Although it was nice to have Mark Ellege as a friend, but she still couldn't help wishing he were more than that. At least conversation between them was becoming less strained. "Well, thank you. I really appreciate that. I know Danny and Sophie will be thrilled."

"They're great kids, Lauren."

It was so nice to see that, despite the discomfort prevalent over the past week, a natural flow of conversation ensued. Lauren went to bed feeling hopeful that night and relieved to know Danny and Sophie would be well taken care of.

★ ★ ★

Mark was looking forward to spending the day with Danny and Sophie. Although he hadn't been around small children very much, Danny and Sophie were great kids. Before he left, he took a look at his Constitutional Law textbook and knew he should be spending the day catching up on his reading. Although his studying was still very important to him, his desire to do well in school was momentarily superceded by his wish to spend time with Lauren and her kids. He couldn't think of anything he'd rather do today than spend the day with Danny and Sophie.

He got up early and made sure to be in the kitchen before Charlie came to pick Lauren up. She went over a few details with him and thanked him profusely before leaving. Shortly after she left, Danny and Sophie made it downstairs.

They were dressed and ready for breakfast.

After bowls of cereal, the kids agreed to help Mark wash the car. Since Charlie had taken the Mercedes, they decided to wash the Range Rover that Tara usually drove. They were excited to help him scrub the car and of course couldn't help splashing each other with the water. Mark's mind went back to the last time they had done the chore together. He'd probably only known Lauren for a couple of days. For some reason, the image of Lauren wiggling out of his arms as he tried to grab the water hose from her lingered in his mind. He smiled at the memory of their feet getting tangled in the hose as they fell to the ground. He remembered distinctly the moment they shared as they both lay on the ground, completely soaked. Despite the great effort he'd given to keeping such thoughts out of his mind, they still prevailed.

The past week had been extremely difficult as he tried to put his feelings for Lauren aside. He kept telling himself that it could never work out. Their lives were headed in completely different directions, and they could never make each other happy. Although his mind was firm in that belief, his heart told a different story. Every time he saw Lauren, he wanted to pull her into his arms and recreate the moment they'd shared in the limo. From the look on her face, it was obvious she felt the same way. He could tell she was hurting, but he had to be strong enough for the both of them. Otherwise, one of them would end up getting hurt. As he tried hopelessly to convince himself that it could never work, he was suddenly brought back to the present when Danny splashed him with water.

Mark laughed and ran away from Danny to the other side of the car. They continued the cat-and-mouse game until Mark at last let Danny completely douse him. As they continued washing the car, all three wet from head to toe, he couldn't help but feel love for Danny and Sophie. They were wonderful children and so well-adjusted for the kind of life they led. Lauren had done well to keep them sheltered from her chaotic life. Her love for them was obvious, and Mark didn't doubt that she would do anything for them. There were so many of Lauren's qualities that he admired. If only a few things could be different, he felt quite certain that he could spend eternity with her.

After they all finished changing into dry clothes, Mark parked the Range Rover in the garage and then drove them in his own car to do a few errands, and then they went to have pizza for lunch. Both children were well behaved and respectful. Even though their mother was wealthy, they didn't seem spoiled. They were amused and impressed by small things and having pizza was actually a treat for them. After lunch, they went to Holmby Park for a few hours. With all schools out for spring break, it seemed that children were in abundance everywhere they went.

Mark felt exhausted at the park, and it was only three o'clock. The children were full of energy and didn't seem to tire at all. He was able to convince them to leave, and they took a trip to San Fernando Valley to pick up a few cheap games at Wal-Mart. He was surprised that they didn't know how to play checkers and even more surprised at how much they liked Wal-Mart. Apparently, Lauren never took them to Wal-Mart, and they were impressed by the simple trip.

The children kept him busy for the rest of the afternoon as he showed them how to play checkers. Then they all took turns playing against each other. During their games, he realized how sad it was that Danny and Sophie were growing up without a dad. Although Lauren more than made up for it with her outpouring of love and attention, they still needed a father. A father should have been washing the car with them and showing them how to play checkers. Nevertheless, he felt privileged to be able to share the day doing those things with them. He glanced at his watch and was startled to see how fast the day had gone. It was already time to pick Lauren up. Danny and Sophie were both very eager to see their mom, and suddenly Mark felt the same way.

15.

Exhausted was not a strong enough word to describe how Lauren felt. Gus had overdone it, but they were able to wrap up the on-location shoot and wouldn't have to fly back to Catalina. Lauren didn't care if it was years before she saw Catalina Island again. Although she was tired, her excitement at seeing Mark and the kids was more pronounced. She was a little surprised to see Mark pull up in his Nissan, but it didn't really matter. Danny and Sophie greeted her with overexuberant hugs and took turns filling her in on the details of their day. Lauren glanced over at Mark several times. Watching him smile at the satisfaction in the kids' voices brought a deep warmth into her heart. She suspected Danny and Sophie weren't the only ones who had enjoyed their day. After every minute detail had been relived, the children settled down into content silence as Mark informed Lauren that they had both behaved extremely well.

"Can we go to McDonald's now?" Danny asked from the backseat. "I'm hungry."

"Me too," Sophie echoed.

Lauren looked at Mark. "You must be tired after a long day. What do you think? I mean, you already took them out for pizza."

He shrugged. "It's okay with me. It is the last day of spring break and then we all have to go back to school," he said, nodding his head toward the kids. "We might as well live it up. That is, if McDonald's food is okay with you?"

She laughed.

"Please, Mom," Danny and Sophie said in unison.

"Okay."

When they reached McDonald's, Lauren instinctively reached for the glove compartment. "Sorry, I was just going to get my hat. I forgot we're in your car. Being recognized at McDonald's would be like the worst."

Mark smiled and pulled off his Lakers baseball cap. He brushed a hand through his hair and then placed the cap over Lauren's head, taking a moment to adjust it.

"A Lakers hat?" she asked.

"Why not?"

"I hate the Lakers."

"At least you won't be recognized."

"But if I am, then people will think I'm a Lakers fan."

"And?"

"And I hate the Lakers," she repeated.

"Does it really matter?"

"I guess not," she groaned, opening the car door.

Mark laughed as he got out and walked with Lauren and the children into McDonald's.

Of course, Lauren wanted to pay but didn't want to insult Mark. It was just McDonald's, so she him. Mark asked her what she wanted and then suggested she find a quiet table in a corner, away from any others who could potentially recognize her. As she watched Mark with Danny and Sophie ordering Happy Meals, she felt so content with the image. What would it be like to be a part of a regular family that went to McDonald's? To be the wife of Mark Ellege in such a family would be unbelievable.

They leisurely ate their dinner then the children played in the play area. Conversation between Mark and Lauren had improved since their fateful talk about just being friends. They had actually become friends, and it felt good.

They finished up dinner and Mark drove them home. As they were getting out of the car, Lauren once again thanked Mark for watching the kids and for dinner. She noticed she still had his Lakers cap on.

"Oh, thanks for the hat. It sure did the trick," she said, taking it off to give back to Mark. She combed her fingers through her hair. Mark took the hat from her and put it in his car.

"Mom, Mark showed me how to play checkers. Mark, can we play one more game before I go to bed?"

Lauren looked at Mark. "You must be tired. You don't have to if you don't want to."

He shrugged. "I don't mind, if it's okay with you."

"Okay, Danny. One game and then it's bedtime."

"All right! Let's go, Mark. I bet I'll win this time."

Mark and Lauren followed the kids up the stairs to the family room. Danny hurried to take out the checkerboard and started setting up the pieces. "Can I be black again?" he asked.

"Sure. You're setting mine up too?"

"Yeah. Can I go first?"

"You bet."

Lauren sat on the couch and watched as Mark sat across from Danny on the floor, playing checkers. Sophie came over with a board game in hand.

"Mommy, will you play Candy Land with me?"

Lauren obliged, and as she played with Sophie, she couldn't help but wish that it could be like this every night. She scolded herself as she began to wonder once again what it would be like to be married to Mark. She couldn't let her mind dwell on what would never be. As she watched Mark play with her son, he looked up and caught her eye. He smiled, and she had to quickly look away before getting any more impossible ideas about marriage to Mark.

The games finished within minutes of each other. They put the games away, and Lauren told them it was time for bed.

"Will you read my bedtime story, Mark?"

Mark looked at Lauren. "If it's okay with your mom."

"Okay, Danny, but go put on your pajamas first."

Danny raced into his room and was back within minutes with *The Cat in the Hat* in hand. He took a seat next to Mark on the couch and Lauren went into Sophie's room to read her a book. After reading *Snow White* for the tenth night in a row, she listened as Sophie said a short prayer. Lauren kissed Sophie and stepped back into the family room. Mark was finishing the story, and Danny seemed like he was in heaven. How much he needed a male figure in his daily life—someone like Mark.

"I'll tuck you in, Danny," Lauren said, taking his hand.

"Okay," Danny said, standing up. "Thanks for everything today, Mark." Danny gave Mark a hug and then bounded into his room.

Lauren smiled. "I'll be right back," she said as she walked into Danny's room. She was thankful to see Mark was still sitting on the couch when she came back.

"Can we talk for a few minutes?" Mark asked, still seated on the couch.

Lauren nodded and walked slowly back to the couch to sit next to him.

Mark cleared his throat and shifted his body slightly to look at her. "The other day when we talked about just being friends—well, I didn't mean it and I don't think you did either."

Lauren's eyes widened. He sure got right to the point. "I don't want you to feel pressured into taking our friendship to another level, not if you're not completely comfortable with it."

"Stop telling me what you think I want to hear," he said, taking her hand. "Please, tell me how you feel."

"I like having you as my friend, Mark, and I don't want to do anything to ruin that, but at the same time, I can't help but want more. I feel like you're holding back and I can understand that. So, while every time I see you, I want so desperately for you to kiss me again, I don't want anything to happen to our friendship." She hadn't meant to open her heart up to him like that, but it had been foremost on her mind every day.

Mark moved in closer. "I want to be with you, Lauren," he said, closing the gap between them. He leaned in toward her and kissed her lips. Putting his arm around her back, Mark pulled her closer to him and Lauren slipped her arms around his neck. His kiss lifted her faltering spirit and filled a void within her that had been empty for too long.

Finally pulling away to catch her breath, Lauren whispered, "I've wanted that for so long."

"I didn't know," he said, caressing her cheek.

Lauren closed her eyes and pulled herself into him. "I didn't think you'd want to be with someone like me."

"Someone like you?" he asked, looking into her eyes.

"I've been away from the Church for so long. I'm doing everything I can to make things right again, but I still have a long way to go. You've probably never faltered."

"I'm not perfect, Lauren. None of us are. That's why we have the Atonement and we can repent."

"I know, but I've done so many things to repent for."

"But you're working on it, and I admire that about you. Let's just take it one step at a time. Right now, the only thing I want to think about is kissing you again," he said as he leaned in toward her.

Lauren didn't argue with that. She couldn't think of anything else she'd rather be doing than kissing Mark. It was what she had been thinking about since that night—which had seemed like the most perfect night ever. Tonight was a very close second.

16

The following morning, Mark hurriedly showered and got dressed. This time he didn't hesitate when he turned the doorknob and hurried down the garage steps into the kitchen. The fleeting doubts he'd been feeling the last time were gone. Now he felt surety in his heart when he thought about being with Lauren.

Mark walked into the kitchen to find Danny and Sophie finishing their breakfast. Danny announced that their mom was taking a shower. Mark joined them for breakfast and waited for Lauren to come down. His heart began beating fast in anticipation of seeing her again. The encounter the previous night was still fresh in his mind and the tender emotion Lauren had awakened in him was still present.

As she walked into the kitchen moments later, Mark fought to keep himself from rushing over to her. He didn't want to create an awkward situation in front of the kids. Hopefully, she would explain it to them later and then he wouldn't have to restrain himself from taking her into his arms. The smile she flashed him as she walked toward the table told him she was feeling the same way.

"Good morning, Mark."

She looked so beautiful; Mark could scarcely take his eyes off her. Although she was dressed simply in blue jeans and a bright red scoop-neck T-shirt, Lauren looked stunning. Her honey-blonde hair hung loosely down her shoulders with a few wisps of hair framing her face. "Hi, there. How are you this morning?"

"Very good," she said, smiling at him. She kissed Sophie and Danny on the forehead as she moved across the room to the refrigerator. She poured a glass of orange juice and then took the seat next to Mark.

"Don't I get a kiss too?" Mark asked.

Both children giggled and watched the two adults expectantly.

Lauren turned to him in amazement. He hadn't meant to say it out loud, but now that he had, he hoped the children wouldn't get the wrong idea.

Before Mark knew it, she leaned over and kissed his forehead. Her kiss was followed by unrestrained giggles from Danny and Sophie.

"Thank you," Mark said.

"So, what are your plans today?" Lauren asked him as she took a drink.

"I don't really have any. What are you doing?"

"I don't know," Lauren said, turning to the children. "What do you guys want to do today?"

"Can Mark take us fishing? He was telling us about fishing on the pier and I've never been fishing. Can we go today?" Danny asked.

Lauren raised an eyebrow as she turned her attention to Mark. "Fishing?"

"I was just telling him sometimes I go down to the beach and fish off the pier."

"Would you like to go fishing, Sophie?" Lauren asked.

"Yeah! Can I have my own pole? I don't want to share with Danny."

Lauren looked back at Mark. "I guess we're going fishing if that's okay with you."

"Sounds great. I'll get my pole; we can rent the other poles down by the pier."

They spent most of the day at Santa Monica Beach, first fishing and then walking along the shore. Mark couldn't remember ever having such a good time at the beach. Sharing the day with Lauren and the children had been truly fulfilling. He imagined that's what it would be like to be a family. Doubts that he had previously had about a possible relationship with Lauren were gone. It just felt right.

Helping Lauren tuck Danny and Sophie into bed that night after they returned from dinner felt right too. As he read Danny a bedtime story in his room, he could feel the little boy reaching out to him, needing and wanting his love. It felt so good to have a small child look up to him and admire him the way Danny did. Lauren came in to kiss Danny good night just as Mark finished the story. As Mark listened to Danny say a short, but heartfelt prayer, he felt the Spirit present, giving him the needed assurance that this was where he was supposed to be. Danny expressed gratitude, not only for his mother and sister, but also for Mark. Hearing Danny's sincere prayer touched him more than anything he could remember. After the prayer, Lauren turned off Danny's light and closed the door. Mark took her hand and together they walked into the family room.

Mark immediately wrapped his arms around Lauren, and pulled her close. "I've been waiting all day to do this," he whispered in her ear and then he kissed her lips. It was several minutes later when he finally pulled away.

"Well, it was worth the wait," Lauren said. "At least, it was for me."

Mark smiled and smoothed her hair away from her face. "For me, too."

"Thank you for today. I had such a wonderful time with you and I know Danny and Sophie had a blast."

"I did too, you know."

Lauren smiled and wrapped her arms around his waist. She pulled herself closer into his embrace. "It feels so good to be in your arms."

Mark kissed the top of her head and agreed with her. Although he didn't want the night to end, Mark finally pulled himself away and they both agreed it was probably a good time to say good night. They did a little more kissing at the foot of the stairs as Lauren walked him to the door. As he gave her a final kiss, he wondered how he would survive until tomorrow.

On Sunday, he drove Lauren and the kids to church, happy and willing to do so while Tara was out of town. Driving to church that morning once again confirmed the feeling he had the previous two nights. Being with Lauren, getting closer to her and her children, was the right decision for him. He wondered how he could have ever doubted it. Danny and Sophie didn't seem to notice or mind when Mark took Lauren's hand and held it for most of sacrament meeting. They got a few curious glances during the course of the meeting, but it didn't seem to faze Lauren. She was used to being watched on a frequent basis and had obviously learned to ignore it. However, for Mark it felt more uncomfortable. He felt as though people were wondering about their sudden closeness. In the end, it didn't matter. All that mattered was how he felt about Lauren. He was beginning to care about her with increased intensity and, in his heart, he felt it was how it should be.

After church, the four of them were in high spirits. The feelings left over from the morning spent at church, coupled with his contentment in being with Lauren and her kids, left Mark completely happy. He suspected the others felt the same.

At home, Mark insisted they make Sunday dinner together. He was quite impressed with Lauren's culinary skills. Although she said she hadn't cooked in years, her baked ziti and homemade garlic bread were delicious. He was amused at the fact that she had difficulty in locating everything in her own kitchen. She again pointed out the fact that she hardly ever cooked, thanks to Meredith. The children were eager to help, and Lauren let them take turns grating cheese.

After dinner, they spent the better half of the evening playing games in the upstairs family room. Once again when bedtime came around, Mark felt joy in helping Lauren put Danny and Sophie to bed. She seemed to enjoy his help and he was beginning to realize how natural it felt to read Danny a bedtime story. Although it seemed to Mark that Sophie enjoyed his company, she still preferred to have her mother read the bedtime story. He suspected that she was very attached to her mother and it was, in fact, Danny who really needed a man in his life at that point. And Mark felt perfectly content to be that man and give Danny the masculine attention he had been deprived of for most of his life.

After both children had been put to bed, Mark repeated his actions from the night before and took Lauren into his arms. It seemed he couldn't get enough of kissing her. After several moments spent showing her how much he enjoyed kissing her, he finally pulled himself away.

"We should probably go downstairs and make a dent in that mess we left in the kitchen," Mark said, not making an attempt to release her.

"You're probably right. We shouldn't leave it for Meredith. She might have a heart attack when she sees that I cooked."

Mark laughed. "We can do it together."

In the kitchen, as Mark rinsed the dishes and handed them to Lauren, she placed them in the dishwasher. Something as simple as loading a dishwasher together seemed to intensify the feeling he had felt all weekend. They were meant to be together. He could see it in Lauren's face that she felt the same way.

Mark turned the water off after the dishwasher was completely loaded. He wiped his hands on a dishcloth. "I was thinking, if you wanted to, on Tuesday, the Jazz are in town to play the Lakers. Do you want to go?

"I feel sorry for your Lakers."

Mark laughed. "I wouldn't start any trash talk. The Lakers have the best record in the NBA right now."

"Well, we'll see. I would love to go and see the Jazz. I can't remember the last time I saw them play."

"Okay, good. It will be fun."

"I'll have Kim make arrangements."

"Uh, Lauren, when a man asks a woman out, he kind of would like to make the arrangements himself."

"Right, I'm sorry. I'm just so used to it. In Hollywood, dating is pretty much all arranged by personal assistants. But it is nice dating someone not in the biz. Sometimes, when I'm around you, I actually feel like a normal person. You know, someone who makes dinner, washes dishes, goes fishing," she said with a laugh. "I kind of miss that. Thank you for bringing some normalcy to my life."

"Thanks. I think that was a compliment. You kind of make me sound very boring and unglamorous."

Lauren laughed. "I didn't mean it that way. I meant it as the highest of compliments. I really love being with you. Doing something as mundane as washing dishes brings me so much joy, just because it's with you."

Mark smiled. He knew what she meant. He leaned in close to her and kissed her. As they stood together, he felt in his heart that being with her was the right thing. It had never felt more right than this.

The next day was spent in much the same manner. Mark felt a continued sensation that being with Lauren was right. He met her and the kids for breakfast in the morning before they dispersed for the day. The day didn't seem to go fast enough and he rushed to meet her at the studio. Lauren had given Meredith a few more days off while her son recuperated, so

Mark took her to get the kids and then they went to pick up Chinese food. At home, they shared the simple dinner together and once again Mark felt a confirmation that he wanted them to be a family. *We should be having dinner together every night,* he thought.

The next day after dinner, Tara was finally home and stayed with the kids while Mark took Lauren to the Lakers game. She was dressed in blue jeans and a white, collared shirt. She looked perfect wearing her Jazz baseball cap, with her hair loosely hanging down her shoulders. Mark put his Lakers hat on, and they teased each other about which team was better.

Mark had bought the best tickets he could afford. The Lakers were having a good season and tickets were in demand. He had to buy them through a ticket broker because the season was sold out, so he ended up paying over two hundred dollars for each ticket. That was much more than he would ever spend on a sporting event or even a date, but he didn't want Lauren to have to sit in the nosebleed section, which is where he usually sat. Despite the big price tag, the tickets weren't even that good, probably higher up than she was used to sitting. Stars like Lauren usually sat courtside, but those tickets were out of his price range. He felt bad about not being able to treat her the way she was accustomed to, making him doubt once again whether they should be together. But something told him that it didn't really matter to her. If she wanted to date a man who could afford to sit on the floor next to Jack Nicholson, she could easily find him, but here she was with Mark. And he was pretty sure that was where she wanted to be.

Mark felt more comfortable taking his own car. Driving the Mercedes made him feel like he was working. He felt more at ease in his Nissan. They parked in the already-crowded lot and he took Lauren's hand as they walked into the Staples Center.

Hearing the music blare over the loudspeaker as the teams warmed up on the court always set the tone for a basketball game. It was wonderful to have a girlfriend who loved basketball, even if it was the Jazz. He was actually enjoying the joking rivalry with Lauren. As they walked toward their seats, Mark was irritated to see that the tickets were even worse than he had expected. He couldn't believe he'd paid that much for these tickets.

Lauren didn't seem to notice or mind as she took her seat. "It's been years since I've seen the Jazz play. I can't believe how much the team has changed."

Mark handed her the program he'd bought. "Yeah, sorry to say, they're not as good as they used to be."

"We'll see," she said, elbowing him in the ribs. She took the program and began leafing through it.

Through most of the first quarter, the Lakers dominated. He almost felt sorry for Lauren. The Jazz really weren't what they used to be, and against his Lakers they had almost no chance. He voiced his thoughts and they continued a teasing, friendly banter for the first half.

During halftime, Mark watched as a teenage girl shyly approached their seats. "Excuse me, Ms. Olsen, can I have your autograph?"

Lauren smiled. "Sure," she said, taking the program the young girl proffered her. "So, are you a Lakers fan?"

"Yeah," the girl said, seeming unsure of Lauren's reaction.

"Good choice." Mark couldn't help but put in his two cents.

Lauren frowned. "But, you like the Jazz too, right?"

"Yeah," the girl said, absolutely beaming that Lauren was having a conversation with her.

Lauren finished signing her name and then handed the program and pen back to her. "Enjoy the game."

"Thank you so much. I'm such a huge fan. You're, like, the best!"

"Thanks. That's nice of you," Lauren said, smiling.

Mark took her hand and kissed it. "You're so nice."

"She was cute, even though she likes the Lakers."

Mark laughed. He wasn't laughing twenty minutes later as the twelfth autograph seeker approached Lauren. It seemed like the shy teenage girl and Lauren's gracious response to her had opened the floodgates for the fans. Mark didn't mind those who came at halftime, but once they started coming to ask for autographs during the game, he began to get annoyed. It seemed so rude; didn't they realize she was trying to watch the game? Lauren was far too nice because she didn't say anything, she just kept signing.

Finally, the crowd around them died down and they were able to watch the rest of the game. Mark suspected that he enjoyed the game more than Lauren because the Lakers blew out the Jazz. Lauren had stayed optimistic throughout the entire game, but even with their loss, she still seemed to enjoy herself.

"I'm sorry about your Jazz," he said, turning to kiss Lauren lightly on the lips.

"It's okay. I guess it's really a rebuilding year."

Mark smiled at her optimism. They waited for the crowds to disperse a little before he led her toward the exit. They followed the crowd outside and as Mark neared his car, he could see a group of people gathered around it.

Lauren stopped suddenly. "Oh great, your car is surrounded by paparazzi."

"How did they know that was my car?"

"They've got eyes and ears everywhere. One of them finds a scoop and before you know it, they're all here."

"Let's go get security," Mark said, and he turned around to walk back toward the arena.

Mark talked to a security guard, who agreed to accompany them to his car. As they approached, cameras began flashing and Mark started getting infuriated. Couldn't they just go to a basketball game without it having to grace the cover of some tabloid? The ruthless cameramen ignored the security guard as he asked them to get away from the vehicle. The cameras continued flashing, only a few of the photographers stepping away.

Mark and Lauren were able to make their way into his car, but it was still surrounded by several paparazzi. A few of the more assertive ones even aimed their cameras right into the car windows. Mark could hear the security guard yelling a few threats toward the cameramen if they did not step away from the vehicle. Finally, after several more minutes of struggling, Mark was able to ease his car out of the spot and followed a long line of cars to the exit.

"Are you okay?" he asked, turning to Lauren.

"I'm fine," she said. "How about you?"

"I just can't get over how rude they are. They have no respect."

Lauren frowned. "I know. I guess I'm used to it. It's very rare that I am able to go anywhere without someone recognizing me."

Mark shook his head. "I don't know how you could ever get used to something like that."

"I don't like it, but really, I have no choice. It's just something I have to live with."

Mark didn't know how she had learned to live with it. He couldn't imagine not being able to go anywhere without such a commotion. He had been with her on several occasions when such a situation had presented itself, but for it to happen on a daily basis was unthinkable.

When he pulled up in front of the house, his anger had dissipated and he was feeling more at peace, just as he had earlier that day. He parked the car and walked Lauren to the door. Impulsively, he took off his baseball cap and put it on backwards. Then he leaned in toward Lauren, taking her cap off as he kissed her. He kissed her several more times as she put her arms around his neck, pulling herself closer to him.

He kissed her once more before speaking. "Thanks for coming with me tonight. I had such a good time with you."

She smiled. "I don't even care that the Jazz lost, I loved being with you," she said as she kissed him.

"I was thinking, if you're not doing anything this

weekend, I would love to take you and the kids to San Diego."

"That sounds wonderful."

"I want you to meet my parents. My mother is a big fan. She's dying to meet you."

"Really? Well, I would love to meet them."

"There's a place I want to take Danny and Sophie. There's a model railroad museum that I know Danny would love. And, just next to that is the San Diego Zoo, which I'm sure they would both like."

"They will love it, Mark. It sounds perfect," she said, hugging him. "I'll have Kim arrange for our hotel."

"No—no way. I want you to stay with my parents. Everyone's moved out, so they have plenty of room."

"Are you sure? I would hate to impose."

"Lauren, my mother has been hounding me to introduce you for weeks. She would love to have you and the kids stay there. I would like it too."

"All right. I would love to," she said.

Lauren helped Danny and Sophie finish packing their small suitcases. They were both eager for a road trip and really excited to meet Mark's parents.

The drive to San Diego was all Lauren could ask for. They sang silly songs and played travel games. Danny and Sophie enjoyed themselves thoroughly. They stopped at a pizza place and had dinner on the way. When they pulled up in front of Mark's parents' home, it was getting dark. Lauren could see it was a nice two-story home. The lawn was well manicured. It reminded her a lot of her childhood home in Salt Lake.

As they walked toward the front door, Lauren felt butterflies overtake her stomach. What if Mark's parents didn't like her? What if it didn't go well at all? All sense of nervousness disappeared as a petite woman with a warm smile and shoulder-length gray hair opened the door. Her soft porcelain features were enhanced by her welcoming smile.

Marian Ellege hugged her son and led them inside. Introductions were made, and Marian made them feel at ease. They were joined by Mark's father, Raymond. Lauren liked him right away.

A tall man, he stood over a foot taller than his wife. He was wearing dark blue pants and matching suspenders over his ivory button-down shirt. He bent down to be eye-level with the children. Turning to Danny, he held out his hand and said, "You must be Sophie, and is this your sister, Danny?"

Both children laughed. "No," Danny said. "I'm Danny."

Raymond made a perplexed face. "So, you're Danny. And, her name is Danny too? That's strange."

They laughed again. "No! I'm Danny. Her name is Sophie. She's a girl; her name can't be Danny."

"Oh, okay. I think I've got it now," Raymond said. "Nice to meet you both." He shook their hands and then moved out of the way to allow them into the living room.

"Dad, this is Lauren," Mark said.

Raymond held out his hand and took Lauren's in his. "Did it suddenly get bright in here? I think we have a real star in our midst."

Lauren smiled. "It's nice to meet you."

"Nice to meet you too," he said, turning to the children. "Knock, knock."

"Who's there?" Danny said, laughing already.

"Orange."

"Orange who?" Sophie asked.

"Orange you glad to finally be here?"

"Oh, Raymond," Marian said. "Let them come into the kitchen. Come in, all of you. You must be tired from the drive." She led them into the kitchen. "I'm sure everyone could go for a nice snack."

They sat in the kitchen and had ice cream as they became

acquainted. Lauren started to relax; Mark's parents made her feel welcome, asking her questions about herself and the children. Marian repeatedly told her what a great fan she was and how much she loved Lauren's movies. As the night progressed, Lauren could tell that the children were growing weary.

Marian took them upstairs. "I love having company, so I keep bedrooms ready at all times. Michele, Mark's older sister, lives in Irvine with her family. They come down a lot to stay with us. My other son lives near Las Vegas with his family and they come stay with us sometimes too. So, we have plenty of space. I'm so glad you came to stay."

"Thank you for having us," Lauren said, following Marian down the hallway.

"It's my pleasure, dear. Do you think the kids would mind sharing a room?" she asked. "There are bunk beds in here." Marian led them inside one of the rooms.

"This will be great. Thank you."

"Your room's right next door. Do let me know if you need anything," she said. "I'll let you get settled."

Lauren closed the door behind her and helped Danny and Sophie prepare for bed. She told them to get some rest since they had a full day tomorrow. They didn't argue, both seeming worn out from the trip. She tucked Danny into the top bunk and Sophie into the bottom after their prayer.

Lauren went back downstairs where Mark and his parents were congregated in the family room. Mark patted the spot next to him on the couch and Lauren took the seat beside him. He took her hand and greeted her with a smile. "Are the kids all settled?"

Lauren nodded. "I'm sure they fell right asleep."

"Oh, they'll have so much fun tomorrow," Marian said. "I wish you were staying longer. There's so much to do here for kids."

Raymond interjected. "There's Sea World, the children's museum, the beach. I think they would like all of that."

Lauren smiled at the idea that the Elleges were wishing

to take Danny and Sophie to all those places. "They'd love all those things."

"Well, Mark will just have to bring you down more often," Marian said, smiling at her son.

Mark smiled back and squeezed Lauren's hand. They spent the next hour talking. Lauren got to know Mark's parents better and felt like she loved them already. They reminded her a lot of her own parents. After so many years, they were still affectionate with each other. Raymond kept his arm around his wife the entire time they sat together. Several smiles passed between them during the conversation. It was exactly what Lauren imagined it would be like after thirty years of marriage to Mark. She wondered if marriage would be possible between them. Things looked really good now; she just hoped it would last.

The next morning, Lauren woke up to an overwhelming aroma coming from the kitchen. She showered and dressed and then went downstairs to find Danny and Sophie cracking eggs with Marian.

"I'm sorry I slept in," Lauren said.

"Don't you worry about a thing, dear. Your two little ones are great helpers."

"Look, Mom. Mrs. Ellege is letting me help her make scrambled eggs."

"I see that. And, you're helping too, Sophie?"

Sophie smiled. "I get to pour the pancakes."

"Well, what can I do to help?" Lauren asked.

"You can work on these sausage links," Marian said, handing Lauren a fork.

Lauren began moving the sausage around in the frying pan and memories of growing up came flooding back. Every Saturday morning had been like this. The whole family gathered in the kitchen, making breakfast together. Why had she been so quick to turn her back on such happy moments? No moment in her adulthood could compare with the feelings she had during those times her family shared in their small kitchen.

Mark came down shortly, and his father offered a blessing. Eating the meal together felt so much like being with her own family. Was it only an unrealistic dream to want to recreate such a moment with her kids? Could she dare to dream about sharing a family with Mark one day? As she glanced at him across the table, for an instant she felt that he imagined the same thing too.

After breakfast, Mark drove them to Balboa Park where the zoo and the San Diego Model Railroad Museum were located. Danny wanted to go to the museum first and Sophie insisted on the zoo. After a coin toss, it was decided that the zoo would be first. Both children expressed excitement to see the elephants and then moved from the monkeys to the zebras. Neither Danny nor Sophie seemed to tire, but after two hours of walking around, Lauren called for a break. They snacked on nachos and lemonade and walked around for another hour.

A quick lunch of hot dogs followed and then they went to the San Diego Model Railroad Museum, where Danny looked like he'd died and gone to heaven. Lauren knew Sophie wasn't as interested in trains, but she was nevertheless excited for her brother.

Lauren picked up a map of the museum and they walked around to different layouts. Danny had become increasingly interested in model layouts since Mark's Christmas gift.

Danny's eyes lit up and he tugged at Mark's hand, showing him different layouts, pointing out Union Pacific, Santa Fe, and Rio Grande trains. Lauren wondered how she would ever get him out of the museum.

After two more hours of looking at the model trains run along different layouts, Lauren took a tired Sophie into the gift shop, where they found a card game to play while they waited for Danny to get his fill. Mark walked around with the enthusiastic Danny for another hour.

After a half hour in the gift shop, Danny picked out a book, a video showing the model train layouts of the museum, and a new caboose for his own layout at home. Lauren was finally able to convince him to go a little before dinnertime.

Lauren couldn't remember the last time she'd been so exhausted, but she was pleased Danny and Sophie had enjoyed themselves. She had enjoyed herself as well. Spending time with Mark in the semblance of a family was like a lovely dream come true.

When they reached the Ellege home, Marian said that a pizza was on the way for the kids. She had rented a few videos for them and insisted that Mark and Lauren change and go out for a nice dinner. Lauren thought twice about the idea and finally decided to go even though she was so worn out. It would be nice to share a romantic dinner with just Mark. They really hadn't been on that many dates together.

Lauren took a quick shower while Danny and Sophie had pizza with Marian and Raymond. After dressing in a black skirt, ivory-colored blouse, and high-heeled sandals, she went downstairs to find that Danny had talked the others into watching the model railroad layout video. Poor Sophie! She looked so bored. Marian assured her that they would watch her choice of video afterward.

As they walked toward the door, Lauren could hear Raymond's booming voice above the video, telling knock-knock jokes.

Mark looked so handsome in navy slacks and a gray button-down shirt. They walked hand-in-hand out to his car.

Lauren smiled as she got into the car. "Thank you for today. The kids had such a good time. I did too, but I know Danny and Sophie enjoyed themselves so much. They were the perfect places to take them."

Mark reached out to squeeze her hand before starting the car. "I had a wonderful time too. I just love Danny and Sophie. Being with you and the kids today was great. It was obvious how much fun they were having, and I think that's what I enjoyed the most, seeing it all through their eyes."

Lauren smiled. She knew exactly what he meant. As they drove, Lauren looked out the window, watching the sun go down, the flicker of the city lights increasing as the night darkened. They drove downtown to the embarcadero, where they took a ferry to Coronado Island. Lauren remembered coming to Coronado once before when she'd first moved to California. Although it was actually an isthmus, Lauren remembered someone told her it was often referred to as an island because it had the feel of an island. As they stepped off the ferry at the Ferry Landing Marketplace, it felt like something out of an earlier era.

They walked a few blocks to an Italian restaurant. Lauren was impressed with the stellar views of downtown from the windows that stretched from floor to ceiling. What a wonderful view of the moon's cascading light emanating off the ocean waves.

Tables were arranged around the room, facing the window's view. Dark blue linen tablecloths covered the round tables, whose centerpieces were china vases holding fresh cut freesias. Lauren was enjoying the soothing atmosphere and was glad that Mark hadn't chosen one of those trendy eateries in the Gaslight District that were much like the fast-paced restaurants where she was used to eating.

The waiter explained the specials and then gave them a moment to peruse the menus. Lauren settled on grilled shrimp over angel hair pasta and Mark opted for manicotti. As they waited for their dinner to be served, Mark and Lauren sampled the bruschetta. They talked about their afternoon, both laughing as Mark recalled Danny's excitement as he gaped at train layout after train layout.

Once their salads had arrived and the waiter left the table, Mark fixed his gaze on Lauren. "Lauren, do you mind if I ask you something personal? I really hate to ask, but it's something I've wondered for some time."

Lauren put down the slice of bread she had just picked up. Something in Mark's voice cautioned her to get her defenses ready. "What is it?"

"I just wondered how involved Danny and Sophie's father

is in their lives. I've never heard you mention him."

Him? Mark's question and her obvious response to it would no doubt magnify the underlying hint of judgment that his question seemed to carry. Lauren cleared her throat. "Well, for starters, they don't have the same father."

"Oh?"

"I'm sorry. I thought you knew that. It's common knowledge."

Mark frowned and shook his head. "I guess I wasn't aware."

"Does it matter to you?"

He shrugged. "No, not really. I just didn't know."

"Well, getting back to your original question. Danny's father is not involved in our lives at all. We were only married a year before I became pregnant and Victor wasn't happy about it. He wanted me to have an abortion. Of course, I couldn't do that, so we got divorced. Danny's never met his father, which is no great loss. Victor is completely worthless as far as men go.

"Sophie's father is a little different, but not much. We weren't married long, but he was actually thrilled about having a baby—for a little while that is, until the reality set in. Our relationship was not strong enough and his career was just taking off, so it didn't work out. Trevor still keeps in touch. He'll call Sophie once in a while and always sends her a birthday and Christmas present. When he's in town, he will usually come by and see her, but that's only one day a year, maybe."

"Wow. So, you've pretty much done it all on your own."

Lauren nodded. "Yeah, pretty much, but I don't regret any of it. I love Danny and Sophie so much—more than anything. I don't know what I would do without them." She was still feeling uneasy. Was it really okay with him? Didn't it bother him just a little? Lauren was too afraid to ask.

Mark reached across to take Lauren's hand. "I think you're a wonderful mother. They're lucky to have you."

"Thank you. That really means a lot to me."

Their waiter brought over their meals, and the food was as impressive as the atmosphere.

After dinner, a stroll down the still populated streets was a romantic way to end the perfect day. Watching the faint moonlight radiate from the thin sliver of a half-smile proffered by the sky that evening, Lauren couldn't imagine being happier than at that moment.

The ferry ride back to downtown provided its own brand of romance. Standing on the deck with Mark's arm around her and feeling her windblown hair tickling his face was more than Lauren could ask for. Did life get any better than this?

Mark nuzzled her ear and kissed her cheek. "I love you," he whispered in her ear.

Lauren turned around to face him. "I love you too."

Mark smiled and let the cool breeze of the night and the sounds of the water hitting against the ferryboat speak his feelings. After a considerable silence, Mark cleared his throat. "You asked me once why I wasn't married."

Lauren nodded, remembering asking him the question. Although she'd only asked him once, she had wondered about it a hundred times.

"My brother got married right after his mission. He'd only finished one year of college and so they were pretty broke. He worked in a grocery store while he was going to school. Kristen, his wife, was miserable the entire two years they were married. She wanted to buy a house. Of course, they couldn't afford it. She wanted a new car, expensive clothes. She was never satisfied with what he earned. Kristen had a best friend who married a guy several years older, so her friend, Judy, had it all. Judy's husband made pretty good money, had his own business, and he bought her everything she wanted. Kristen constantly complained about not having enough money, always comparing herself to Judy and what they had. I know my brother struggled with it. He was so hard on himself because he couldn't give Kristen what she wanted, but he was doing his best. They eventually divorced. It was a good thing that they didn't have any children." Mark sighed. "Well, anyway. I just didn't want to end up like that, so I postponed serious dating. I wanted to make sure that I finished school and had a good job so I could support my wife."

Lauren touched his cheek. "Not every woman is like Kristen. My sisters all married young. None of their husbands had finished college and they all saw some pretty rough times. 'Living off love,' that's what Liesel always called it. It didn't matter to them that they didn't have money. They helped put their husbands through college and stuck it out."

"I guess those guys were lucky."

"I guess I'm the lucky one that you wanted to wait to get married. If you were married now, I wouldn't be here with you."

Mark smiled and embraced Lauren tightly, kissing her. The ferry ride was over too soon as far as Lauren was concerned. Before she knew it, they were driving back to Mark's house. Even if she had tried to, Lauren would not have been able to think of a more perfect day. Being with Mark and the kids, almost like a family, had been like a dream. Meeting and loving his parents had been amazing. Ending up in his embrace with his softly whispered words, "I love you," was truly a miracle.

After their trip to San Diego, it was difficult to get back into the routine of things. Lauren's thoughts were focused on the fact that school would soon be over and Mark would be graduating. What were his plans after graduation? Surely he would not want to stick around as her chauffeur. He had bigger and better plans, but would they include her?

Although Lauren felt confident that Mark truly loved her, lingering doubts still crept into her mind. Could he really marry someone like her, someone who hadn't been virtuous her entire life? It was something they didn't really talk about. Although they spent most of their free time together, the topic of marriage had still not been broached. Lauren thought about it all the time and wondered if Mark did too. Even though he hadn't mentioned it, Lauren could sense that he was committed to her.

Lauren was beyond excited the day Mark asked to visit the set. He was to spend the entire day with her during filming. They arrived a little later than usual, with Lauren forgoing her usual workout with her personal trainer.

Instead, she made it just in time for hair and makeup. Mark sat and watched as Lauren's hair was arranged stylishly for her character, Ivonne, who was a woman embroiled in a blackmail scheme against a powerful senator. As her makeup was being applied, Gus popped his head in to announce a wardrobe change.

The scene they had planned on taping involved Ivonne's

confrontation with the senator's wife. "Sela has the stomach flu, so we're going to do the office scene."

Lauren winced at the thought of doing the office scene, which involved Ivonne and her boyfriend, the ringleader in the blackmail scheme, played by her costar Kevin. The scene involved heavy kissing between Ivonne and her boyfriend and was not a scene she wanted Mark to witness. "Can't I just run through my lines without Sela here? I'm not prepared for the office scene."

Gus stepped into the room. "We can't waste a whole day on running through lines. We have to film. Take a few minutes to prepare yourself if you need to, but I need you to be ready to go through with the office scene. Kevin's getting into wardrobe already. Sorry for the change, but we can't waste today."

"Why don't we work on the rally scene?" Lauren asked, desperately wanting to change his mind.

Gus shook his head. "Extras aren't in today. That's scheduled for later next week. Office scene. Sorry, Lauren." Gus stepped out of the room and closed the door behind him, terminating their discussion. Lauren resigned herself to the situation as she sat back to allow them to finish her makeup. One of the production assistants went to get Lauren's wardrobe.

After they finished prepping Lauren for filming, Mark escorted her to the set. She introduced him to several of the crew. Mark chatted with one of them as Lauren prepared for the first scene. Lauren's concentration was off and she fumbled a line and then missed a stage direction on the second take. After several takes, Gus was finally happy with it.

They moved on to the kissing scene, and Lauren threw Mark an anxious look. He smiled encouragingly. She probably should have prepared him for what they would be filming, but had decided against it. Lauren, playing Ivonne, stepped through the senator's door where Kevin, who played her boyfriend, had been searching through the senator's desk. Kevin turned around to face her, surprised by her presence. As she closed the door behind her, Kevin walked toward her. Placing both hands on her face, he drew Ivonne close to him and pressed his lips firmly on hers. He kissed her passionately and Lauren felt herself stiffen.

"Cut," Gus said. "Lauren, I want you to grasp his arms as he starts to kiss you."

Lauren nodded, hesitating to look in Mark's direction. She did not even want to see his reaction. After the third take, she finally hazarded a glance toward Mark. His jaw was clenched tightly and his arms were crossed in front of him. Why did Kevin have to choose today, of all days, to mess up his lines so many times? The scene had to be re-shot several times, but it was finally to Gus's liking. The break for lunch couldn't have come at a better time.

Mark walked quietly with Lauren to her dressing room. They had filled their plates at the catering table and sat at a small table in her dressing room.

Lauren anxiously took a bite of her lemon-pepper chicken. After thorough chewing and swallowing, she cleared her throat. "I'm sorry about that."

Mark only shrugged.

"Are you upset with me?"

Mark took a drink of the bottled water he had been clutching in his left hand. "Why wouldn't I be upset? I just spent an hour watching my girlfriend kissing another guy and there wasn't a thing I could say about it. Worse than that, it's being filmed with a guy yelling, 'Cut, let's do it again.' Over and over again. And you're even asking me if I'm upset about it?"

Whoa, he wasn't just upset. He was mad! "I'm sorry, Mark. That's my job. Besides, it wasn't the scene I thought we were going to film. I wouldn't have invited you today if I knew we were doing that scene."

Mark laughed, only there was no humor to it. "So, it would be okay if I wasn't here?"

"That's not what I meant. It just would have been less uncomfortable for us."

173

"So, you feel more comfortable about kissing other men when I'm not here?"

Lauren shook her head. Nothing she was saying was coming out right. "Mark, you know what I mean. It's not like you didn't know this is part of my job. You've seen my movies. In some of them, I've had to kiss someone. It's a storyline, but kissing is part of it sometimes. I'm sorry if you don't like that, but it's what I do."

Mark sighed and put down the fork he'd been arbitrarily moving food around his plate with. "I know that, but I think it's only natural for me to be upset." He reached over to take Lauren's hand. "I love you. I can't stand seeing another guy kiss you. It makes me crazy. I'm sorry, but that's the truth. I guess it's really different when you're doing it right in front of me."

"I know."

"I love you so much."

"I know. I love you too, Mark. That's why it's so hard to see you angry with me."

He stroked her cheek. "I'm not angry with you. It's that guy you were kissing. I'd like to punch his lights out."

Lauren laughed.

"I'm kidding. I don't want to punch his lights out. I just wish things were different."

"Different how?"

"I wish you didn't kiss men for a living."

"Don't say it that way. I don't kiss men for a living. I'm an actress. I act. Kissing's only part of it. And that part is over for today, so don't let it ruin our day. There's no more kissing today."

"No more kissing today?" Mark asked, leaning in toward her.

"Well, no more pretend kissing," she said, leaning in to meet his lips. They kissed and Lauren wished she could explain to him how different it was to kiss when she was acting. The feeling that overcame her when Mark's lips touched hers couldn't compare to the empty feeling of kissing during a scene.

"We're going to have to talk about this again. If we're going to be together, I just don't know how to accept this as part of our future."

He was talking of the future. He wanted a future with her. It brought her a great deal of joy to know he was thinking of her as part of his future. "Well, we can look through scripts together and decide what's right."

As he kissed her again, she didn't care about future films. At one point in her life, the next film had always been on her mind. She looked for scripts that would be good leading-lady material. Lauren had always wanted to find a part that would bring her to the forefront, make her an acclaimed actress. Suddenly, it didn't matter. Only being with Mark mattered at that moment.

★ ★ ★

Mark pulled into 7-Eleven and filled up the Mercedes. He went inside to pay and grabbed a Snickers for himself and a bag of plain M&M's for Lauren. As he waited in line to pay, he wondered if she would still need him to pick her up once her driving privileges were restored in a few weeks. He would miss picking her up every day at the set. They shared terrific conversations, and Mark would miss those moments if she started driving herself to work every day.

Mark moved up in line and shook his head as he noticed that Lauren's picture graced another cover of a tabloid. As he took a closer look, he grabbed the magazine and slammed it on the counter as he paid the attendant. Shaking his head as he walked back to the car, Mark felt that this scenario somehow seemed familiar. Only this time, it was not him on the cover with Lauren.

Mark drove several miles over the speed limit as he approached Culver City. Something close to rage seethed within him. As he reached a red light, he picked up the magazine and studied it once more. He remembered that day; it was only last week. Mark had dropped her off at the Ivy for a business lunch. He had really liked the way she looked in a dark gray skirt and ivory blouse. Mark had complimented her on how beautiful she looked. And, here she was, seated at a table with her ex-flame, Julian. Whoever had taken the pictures had captured what looked to be an intimate lunch between the pair. The captions to the pictures and the story that followed recounted the couple's initial romance and suggested that they were rekindling that romance. It cited several sources that told about the couple's desire to be together again. Did she take him for a fool?

Mark heard an impatient horn blare behind him and he threw the tabloid against the dashboard as he stepped on the gas. Minutes later, he was parked outside the studio, waiting for Lauren. He shook his head as he remembered the last time he had been in the studio. Watching the woman he loved kissing another man and not being able to do or say anything about it had been disgraceful. What had he been thinking when he decided to get involved with Lauren? She simply was not the kind of woman who a man deeply rooted in the gospel could marry. And, here she was, proving it again.

It angered him to see Lauren emerge from the building with an overzealous smile. Of course she was happy; she had fooled him. By the time she opened the door and sat next to him, he was fuming. He could hardly speak, so he chose not to. If he even opened his mouth, his anger would erupt.

Lauren leaned over and kissed him on the cheek. "Hey there, handsome. How was your day?"

Mark didn't even look at her. He only shrugged his shoulders.

"Everything okay?" she asked, placing her hand on his arm.

"Let's talk about it later," he managed to say in the most even tone he could muster. He shifted into drive and started out of the lot.

"What's the matter, Mark?"

Mark refused to look at her. "I said I would rather talk about it later. I'm too angry to speak right now."

"Has something happened?" she asked, beginning to look alarmed.

Mark finally looked at her and then shook his head, but still said nothing.

"Mark?"

He finally turned to her. "Can you give me some space, here? I am trying to control my anger so I can talk calmly about this with you."

"Mark, you are starting to scare me. Please tell me why you're so angry."

Mark continued to drive toward the house with Lauren pleading with him to tell her what had happened. He refused to until they reached the house. He put the car in park and then let out a long sigh. Picking up the tabloid magazine from where it lay on the dashboard, he handed it to her.

Lauren shook her head. "Kim didn't tell me about this one."

"Does Kim have to do everything for you?" he asked.

"No," she said, "but she usually alerts me if there are blatant lies being told about me in the tabloids." She held the magazine out toward him. "You can't tell me you actually believe this."

Mark shrugged. "I don't know what to believe."

"Well, I am telling you that they are lies. We are absolutely not back together. I have no desire to be with Julian. You believe me don't you?"

Mark turned to face her. "I want to believe you, Lauren, but pictures don't lie. That is you and that is Julian and you are sitting together having lunch, and if I'm not mistaken this picture was taken last week. I remember dropping you off at the restaurant. So while you're having a romantic lunch with your ex-boyfriend, I'm sitting in the car like a schmuck waiting for you."

Lauren shook her head, close to tears. "That's not how it happened!"

"Well, then why don't you tell me how it happened? Can you deny that was just last week? Did you or did you not have lunch with Julian last week and fail to even mention it to me?"

"It was just like I told you. I had a lunch meeting with Rudolph Williams to discuss possible script changes. When I showed up, he had Julian with him. He was hoping to cast Julian in the film as well and wanted to talk to us both. I told him I had no intention of starring with Julian and that if he didn't agree to some very severe script changes, I wouldn't do the film at all. He heard me out, listened to my suggestions, and then turned every one of them down. I told you all that right after the meeting."

"You told me some of that, but you conveniently left out the part about Julian."

"Seeing Julian again was so insignificant for me that I didn't see the point of mentioning it. His presence didn't factor into anything. I have no feelings for him; I actually can't stand the guy. I hardly said a word to him the whole time."

"It's kind of hard for me to believe that you have no feelings for him when only a few months ago, you went out of your way to make him jealous. I remember specifically being involved in that little game," Mark said, with more sharpness than he had intended. "And why isn't Rudolph Williams even in these pictures?"

"Are you trying to say you don't believe that he was even there? Is that how little you trust me?"

"Just answer the question, Lauren. Where's Williams while you and Julian are so cozily having lunch?"

"You know how the paparazzi works. They take dozens of rolls of one subject until they get the exact ones that will sell the most magazines. Rudolph got a few cell phone calls and had to step away from the table. That must've been when they took these pictures. Of course they're not going to put the ones with Rudolph in because that doesn't make for juicy gossip."

Mark took a deep breath and remained silent for a moment. He wanted to believe Lauren, but so many thoughts were going through his mind. The doubts he'd had from the beginning were still ever-present in his mind and he couldn't shake them.

"Mark, don't shut me out. Please say something. Please tell me you believe me. Do you believe me that I didn't know Julian would be there?"

He turned to face her. "I believe you that you hadn't intended on having lunch with Julian. You didn't know he was coming. I believe you that Rudolph was there. I didn't mean to imply that you blatantly lied to me. It's just that . . ." Mark wasn't sure how to say what he was thinking.

"We're from two different worlds. I'm from a world where the only man you kiss is your boyfriend or your husband. You don't have lunch with ex-boyfriends and not tell the man you love. In your world, you kiss other men for a living and having lunch with an ex-lover is so insignificant that you don't bother telling me." He knew he was hurting her, but he had to be honest.

Lauren shook her head, tears slowly streaming down her face. "In my line of work, lunch doesn't mean anything. That's how you do business. Deals get made over lunch. I'm sorry I didn't tell you about Julian, but please don't let that come between us."

"It's not just that. There are so many things. That's only part of it. I don't think I can live with you kissing other men, even if it is for a movie. You make more money in one year than I will ever make in my lifetime. How can you expect me to accept all of these things?"

"It always bothered me that you saw my tithing check."

"Lauren, that's my calling. I can't help it."

"But I knew you would use it against me."

He sighed. "I don't have to see your tithing check to know how much you make. I've seen your house and your cars and your clothes. I see how you live and how different it is from how I live. How can we ever make it work? I'm sorry, Lauren, but I think we were just fooling ourselves when we thought this relationship could work."

"Mark, money doesn't mean that much to me. I was raised the same way you were. I don't have to have a huge house—none of this even means anything to me if I can't have you."

"But it isn't just the money. Don't you see that? It's everything. We're too different. Even if I could get past your job and your money, I don't know if I can ever get past the men you've been with."

"How dare you throw that in my face! I've repented of that. I've taken the necessary steps to get rid of that sin. Who are you to judge me? You're not perfect. None of us is. That's why there is repentance. You should know that, Mr. Returned Missionary."

"I'm just being honest with you about how I feel. I have stayed morally clean my entire life and I always thought that whomever I marry would have done the same. And now I'm faced with the possibility of being with someone who has slept with other men." Mark hadn't intended to be so cruel, but all of the doubts he'd had from the beginning—all of the reasons that had compelled him to not get involved with Lauren—were coming to the forefront.

Lauren angrily wiped away tears. "I can see in your eyes what you think of me."

Mark let out a deep breath. Every word he was saying was like a dagger to her heart. He knew she already regretted her past actions and he was making it worse by bringing it up again, but it really did matter to him. "I'm sorry, Lauren. I don't mean to hurt you," he said, taking her hand. He held it up to his cheek. "I love you so much and that's probably why it's so hard. I want to be with you, but all these doubts keep lingering in my head. I just keep thinking that you've been with other men and I have absolutely no experience. I feel like, if we were to get married, you would always be comparing me to them."

"No, it's not like that. Both my husbands were selfish in every way. They only cared about pleasing themselves. By nature, you are not like that. You're so kind and up until today I never thought you would ever hurt me. I understand you have doubts, but never doubt how much I love you. When I am with you, I think only of you. Those other men mean nothing to me. I was scared to be alone, I felt I needed a man in my life, but I never loved them. No—really. When you kiss me, I feel like you're giving me something. No man I've ever kissed has made me feel that way. They always wanted to take something from me, never give me anything. Yes, you are different because I know that if we were married, you wouldn't be a selfish lover. You would be giving and kind. And for the first time in my life, I actually feel like I deserve that."

Mark brought her hand to his lips and kissed it. "I love you, Lauren, but I need time. I'm sorry. I think I need to leave for a little while."

Lauren nodded and got out of the car. She went around to the driver's side, where Mark got out as well. "That's a good idea," she said. "Go and clear your head. Maybe in a few hours, when you come back, we can talk some more."

Mark took her hand and shook his head. "No, I mean I should go away. Move out for a few weeks."

"What?"

"I'm sorry. I don't mean to leave you without a driver."

"I don't care about a driver, Mark. I need *you*. Please, don't leave."

"I have to. I need some time to think, to figure out what's right. We need some time apart to pray and find out what we want."

"I know what I want."

"Well, I don't. I'm sorry."

"Where are you going to go?" she asked, still crying.

"I don't know. I'll move in with a friend for a few weeks. Finals are coming up soon, and I need time to study. After I graduate, maybe I can think more clearly."

Lauren shook her head; her battle with her tears was over. She stopped trying to fight them back, but furiously wiped them off her face.

Mark took her into his arms and held her for a few minutes. "I'm so sorry. The last thing I want to do is hurt you, but I can't decide anything right now."

"Are you going to say good-bye to Danny and Sophie?" she asked, pulling away from him.

"Maybe you could just explain it to them. I'll call you in a few weeks. I'm sorry. Tell them I'm sorry."

Lauren shrugged. "Don't worry. They'll understand. You're not the first man to walk out on them. I think they've come to realize not to expect too much from men."

"That's not fair. You know I'm not like those other men."

"No, you are different," she said softly. "Because I didn't expect any better from them. I really believed you would never hurt me like this."

"I don't mean to hurt you. I'm sorry. I promise I'm not walking out on you. I'll be back once I've figured everything out."

Lauren looked at him for a long moment and then turned around and walked into the house.

19

It had been two weeks since Mark left and Lauren hadn't heard a word from him. She didn't even know where he was staying; he hadn't bothered to call her. After he left, she hired a car service to do the driving that he regularly did, and Charlie worked extra hours to help make up for Mark's absence. It was ironic though; nobody could make up for his absence. When her driving privileges were restored, it felt strange to once again sit behind the wheel. She started driving herself around more and only used Charlie occasionally, more for his sake than hers. Lauren was sure he wouldn't feel right about accepting his paycheck if he wasn't working, but she decided she preferred driving herself. Nonetheless, she allowed Charlie to drive her to various appointments, all the time wondering how much he knew about the situation. She knew Mark had talked to him just after he left because Charlie seemed to know that Mark wouldn't be around anymore and volunteered to pick up his regular hours.

Brenda's condition had improved slightly, and Charlie seemed eager to work all that Lauren permitted him to. She had been tempted at times to ask if he knew where Mark was, but she would have been too humiliated. Perhaps he knew where Mark was but wasn't saying anything, so Lauren didn't want to put him on the spot.

She realized that graduation had come for Mark and she wondered what he might be doing. He was probably looking for a job or studying for the bar exam. In fact, there were a hundred things he could be doing but calling her apparently wasn't one of them. It almost made her angry. How could he just run out on her without further discussion—and hadn't he promised to call? Periodically she found herself checking the garage apartment to make sure the rest of his belongings were still there. She kept telling herself that he would be back. The majority of his things were still here, and he wasn't the type of person to sneak in and pack up in the middle of the night.

Lauren tried to keep busy during the day so she wouldn't think too much about Mark. At night once Sophie and Danny had gone to bed and everything around her was still, thoughts of Mark and a desire to be with him suffocated Lauren. She longed to be with him and to feel his strong arms around her. It wasn't the first time a man had left her; it was just one of many, but this time was different.

Perhaps it was because she truly loved Mark with a deep and abiding love that would not easily go away. The other men in her life, including both her husbands, hadn't meant as much to her. She had thought she loved them at the time, but now she knew it wasn't real love. With Mark she had tasted true love and actually knew what if felt like to be loved.

This time was different for another reason as well. After her first divorce, Lauren had begun drinking to ease her pain.

The second divorce was much like the first. When the breakup with Nicholas happened, Lauren went over the edge with her drinking. After Julian broke up with her, she became so desperate that she attempted to make him jealous by kissing Mark. All of those acts of desperation had only increased the heartache she had already felt after her breakups. Now she no longer felt a need to turn to those divisive means.

Although this possible breakup was harder than any other, she had the gospel back in her life. That was all she needed to get through this most difficult time of her life. The possibility of losing Mark was real, yet she didn't feel the immediate need to soothe her pain through alcohol. During the times she felt the pain was too unbearable, Lauren turned to her Heavenly Father in prayer. Through constant communication with Him, she was able to feel a certain level of peace she had never felt when she turned to drinking. Now, at those lonely moments of each night when she longed to be with Mark, she prayed and read in the scriptures, sometimes for hours at a time.

Those quiet moments spent at her bedside reading and praying brought her a sense of peace as she prepared for bed each night. Ardent morning prayer soothed her ache and prepared her for a day without Mark. There were so many aspects of her day that reminded her of him. Driving the Mercedes brought to her the most memories, and she was tempted many times to trade it in for a new car. Sitting in her dressing room brought back to mind the day he had spent on the set with her. That day had precipitated the downfall of their relationship. Mark couldn't get past her kissing scene. It was hard for him to accept her lifestyle and it was possible he would never get past it.

Lauren planned to take Danny and Sophie to Salt Lake City the next day for Jacob's graduation. It would do her a world of good to be surrounded by her family and away from the constant and painful reminders of Mark. She realized it had been upsetting for Danny and Sophie too. They had become attached to Mark and were used to seeing him every day. It had been difficult to explain to them why he left and when he was coming back. She had told them that when he graduated, he was going to find a different job and that perhaps he was looking for it. She reminded them that he still cared about them and would call one day to talk to them. She only hoped she wasn't lying to them.

As Charlie drove them to the airport, Lauren tried to focus her mind on more pleasant thoughts. She had decided to buy Jacob a car for his graduation and her father was taking her the next day to help her pick one out to surprise him.

At first, her father had been hesitant, but she managed to convince him that Jacob needed a reliable car to drive to Provo while he attended BYU because he would no doubt want to come home once in a while. She had also told her father that the car would be given to Jacob with the condition that after his first year at BYU, he would sell the car to pay for his mission, with the balance of the money being put in the bank for his return. Once her father had agreed, he became excited to help her pick out the car.

Her father picked them up at the airport and Lauren was anxious to see her family again. She couldn't believe she hadn't been home since Christmas. Danny and Sophie were excited to see their cousins and Lauren hoped it would get their minds off missing Mark. She doubted that would happen for her.

★ ★ ★

Mark walked into Crossroads Mall in Salt Lake City, shaking his head. How could he have forgotten to pack a tie? As he walked toward one of the large department stores, he tried to hurry his pace. He had only an hour before his job interview. At least he was wearing his suit; all that was missing was his tie. He browsed through the men's department, looking for a tie that suggested *serious* and *hardworking*, yet hinted at *witty* and *clever*. How could a tie say all that? Mark shook his head as he struggled to find the right one.

He wondered what he was doing in Salt Lake anyway.

Would he really accept a job here? He still wasn't sure what his
intentions were toward Lauren. He had told himself repeatedly
that the reason he hadn't called her was because he'd been so
overwhelmed with studying for finals, preparing for the bar
exam, and sending out resumes. Although he preferred to stay
in California and had a few interviews lined up for later in the
month, he couldn't pass up the opportunity to interview for
the prestigious Salt Lake firm. An old mission companion had
recommended him, and he felt privileged that they were willing to interview him.

He picked up a solid red tie and held it up against his chest. It
would have to do; he didn't have time to browse around. As he
turned around to walk toward the cashier, he heard his name.

"Mark?"

Mark looked up to see Rich Olsen walking toward him.
"Rich, hi. How have you been?"

"Lauren didn't tell me you were coming too. She told me
you hadn't talked in weeks."

"We haven't. What do you mean, 'coming too'?" Mark
asked.

"Jacob's graduation. Lauren's in town for it. When I saw
you just now, I figured you'd come with her," he said, still
looking bewildered. "But, I guess that doesn't make sense
because my father's at the airport picking her and the kids up
right now."

"No, we didn't come together. In fact, I didn't know she
was coming to Salt Lake. I'm here for a job interview."

"So, I guess it's true. You haven't talked for weeks," Rich
said.

"No, we haven't. I—"

"That's okay," Rich interrupted. "I understand. She told
me why you left and I can understand. I would have a hard time
with her past as well. Don't get me wrong; I love my sister and
she deserves the best, but I can see where you're coming from."

Mark was glad Rich wasn't angry. "I really do love her. I
just need time."

"Well, I think you should tell her that. She's having a really hard time because you haven't called her. Just let her know where your head's at right now."

"I will. I'm just trying to sort some things out right now."

"Well, if you aren't doing anything tomorrow, you should come by the house. We're having a party for Jacob. At least think about it."

Mark hesitated. "I don't know."

"Well, I won't tell Lauren I ran into you. If you decide you want to come, I know everyone would be glad to see you, but if you don't come, then, well, I guess she won't know." Rich took out a page from his planner and wrote down an address.

Mark took the page Rich handed him and folded it in half. "I'm not sure," Mark said.

"Well, I'd better go. I'm looking for a gift for Jacob. I have no idea what to get him. Anyway, good luck with your interview. Hope to see you tomorrow."

Mark waved as Rich walked away. He hurried to pay for his tie and, all of a sudden, felt an added layer to his already flourishing nervousness.

Several hours later, after his interview was over, Mark's sense of anxiety had not decreased in the least. The interview had gone well; one of the partners had clearly stated he was very interested, and he was told he would be hearing from them within the week. So, why was his stomach still in knots? As he drove back to his hotel, he knew he wouldn't be able to relax for the rest of the day, as he had planned. He had unfinished business and he needed to do something about it.

Once inside his room, he pulled his tie off and searched his pants pockets for the planner page Rich had given him earlier that morning. Mark looked at the address. It was only a ten-minute drive. He really needed to go. For some reason, he dreaded the idea of going to Lauren's family get-together. It wasn't that he didn't want to see her; he had missed her greatly. There was a part of him that wanted to seek her out, take her in his arms, and never let go of her—but the other part of him fought the instinct relentlessly. It just wasn't that simple. Of course he loved her, but he still wasn't sure if being together was the right thing for them. That was why he didn't want to—or rather couldn't—face her. Mark didn't have an answer for Lauren yet and he knew that when he saw her, she would demand one. And, quite honestly, he owed her one.

He had tried to call her many times; had even dialed most of the numbers, only to hang up before letting it ring. He wanted to hear her voice, to see her, and to kiss her, but he wasn't ready to fully accept her in his life. Mark knew he wasn't being fair to her; he had promised to call. Sitting in his hotel room, staring at the wall, he had never felt like such a coward.

He wanted Lauren in his life, even felt in his heart that it was right, but he couldn't say it out loud. Deep down, he knew his pride was getting in the way. He was too proud to accept a woman with whom it wouldn't be the first time. After working so hard to graduate and attend law school, he would finally be able to start his career. But, suddenly it didn't matter in the way he had always thought it would. Lauren didn't need to be taken care of the way he had imagined taking care of his wife. She made more money than he; that was something she would never need from him. Had he worked so hard throughout his life to have it not even matter? He just couldn't accept that.

Looking back at his life, he knew pride was what had kept him from ever marrying. He had been so determined to finish school and start a career that he had not seen marriage as a priority. He had wanted to be able to take care of his wife, unlike his brother. Lauren had told him that her sisters had helped put their husbands through school, and he knew many couples who had done the same, but it had never seemed like an option to him. He wanted to be able to take care of his wife. Lisa had broken up with him because he studied too much, but he wouldn't have married her anyway, not until he was able to take care of her. As soon as he secured a job, he would be able to take care of a wife. Ironically, that had been his goal but achieving it was now completely overshadowed by the fact that he didn't need to if he married Lauren. She was able to take care of herself. That was what he couldn't get past. He wasn't sure if he ever would.

The next day, he drove the short distance to South Salt Lake in the rental Pontiac and parked a few houses down from the address Rich had given him. Taking a moment to compose himself, he then looked up to see the house Lauren had grown up in. It was vastly different from what he had imagined. She really had come from humble beginnings. It was a nice, normal house, yet smaller than he had pictured. It was well taken care of, but still, he couldn't envision Lauren living in it. Lauren—the famous Hollywood actress who lived in a huge mansion—actually resided in that house at one point. Mark shook his head as he walked toward it.

He hesitated to ring the doorbell. This wasn't how he had imagined meeting her family. Was it really a good idea? Before he could change his mind, Mark rang the doorbell and waited only a minute before someone opened it. She was a slightly older, somewhat plumper version of Lauren. There was a strong resemblance.

She held the door open and squinted at him. "Mark?"

Somehow, Mark found his voice and held out his hand. "I'm Mark Ellege."

She took his hand. "I recognized you from some pictures Lauren showed me. I'm Rachel. What are you doing here? Never mind, I'm sorry. Please come in." She stood aside and motioned him into the living room.

He looked around the room and saw several men seated in various couches and chairs. They all seemed relaxed and hadn't noticed his entrance. Directly in front of him, Mark noticed a few women bustling in the kitchen. To his immediate left was an open doorway that seemed to lead to the basement, from which an assortment of children's loud voices could be heard.

Before he was able to respond to Rachel's question, which

he hadn't even heard, he caught a glimpse of Lauren emerging from the kitchen.

"Rachel, where did you put the—" Lauren didn't finish her sentence as she stopped midsentence and looked right into Mark's eyes. "Mark."

Mark watched as the woman he loved stood before him, hair pinned up in a bun, wearing a red gingham apron, but more beautiful than ever. "Hi."

"What are you doing here?" she asked, seemingly unable to take another step.

Suddenly they had gotten the attention of the rest of the room. Rich stood up from where he had been reclining in a chair on the opposite end of the room. "Hey, Mark. I'm glad you made it."

Lauren looked from Mark to Rich and gasped. "What's going on here?"

"I ran into Mark at the mall and I invited him over."

Lauren seemed to finally regain the use of her legs and had closed the gap between them. "Why didn't you tell me?" she asked Rich.

Rich smiled mischievously. "I wanted it to be a surprise."

Lauren seemed to relax after Rich's statement. She finally smiled at Mark, obviously past her shock in seeing him. "Well, I'm glad you came. I am really surprised." Lauren looked around the room, for the first time noticing that the rest of her family was watching. "I guess I should introduce you to everyone."

Lauren went around the room and introduced all of the men: her father, brothers, and brothers-in-law. She then stepped into the kitchen and continued with the introductions. Her mother forced a smile and shook his hand, but Mark could feel the tension. Surely Lauren had voiced her anxieties to her family, and Mark could only wonder what they all thought about him. They were engaged in a bit of small talk when a booming voice came from behind him.

"Mark!" Danny exclaimed as he ran toward Mark and jumped into his arms. "I can't believe you're here!"

"Hey, bud. How have you been?"

"Why did you leave? I missed you."

Mark cleared his throat and looked around the room, expectant eyes on him, all waiting for the answer to Danny's question. "Well, you see, I finished school. So, I was taking some time to look for a new job. I had to do some interviews and stuff like that."

"But you already have a job. You work for my mom."

Thankfully, Lauren came to his rescue. "Danny, remember, I told you that Mark is looking for a job as a lawyer. He's not going to be our driver anymore."

"But he's still going to live in our garage, right?"

Mark felt so guilty as Lauren tried to explain the situation to Danny. Although Mark had been well aware that his actions were hurting Lauren, he really hadn't thought about how it was affecting Danny.

After Lauren explained to Danny that Mark still wasn't sure where he was going to live, some of the children were able to lure him back down to the basement with an invitation to play hide-and-seek.

Danny agreed to join their game. Before turning to leave, he looked up at Mark. "Please don't go without saying good-bye."

Mark nodded. "I won't. I promise." He looked at Lauren and she quickly looked away.

"Want to come outside with me and check on the grill?" she asked him.

Mark followed Lauren out the back door to a small fenced-in yard. He watched her flip hamburgers and ribs on the grill. It was a completely different side of Lauren than he'd ever witnessed before. Here, with her family, she just seemed to blend in, not anything like a Hollywood actress.

"I'm sorry I didn't call," he said.

She flipped the last hamburger and then closed the grill. "Why didn't you?" she asked, looking up at him.

Mark sighed. "I don't know. I'm still trying to figure

things out and then with graduation and typing up resumes, I've been overloaded."

"So, what are you doing in Salt Lake?"

"I had a job interview."

Lauren looked up suddenly. "Are you moving here?"

Mark looked away, focusing on his hands. "I don't know. It's a good firm, but they haven't made me a job offer. I'm not sure if I'll take it. I'll probably stay in California, but I thought I should at least do the interview."

Lauren nodded as she busied herself. She opened the grill and started randomly moving the meat around. "I see."

Mark could tell Lauren was upset. He was making all of these plans that didn't include her and it was causing her a great deal of pain.

Lauren closed the lid of the grill and turned to look at him, her eyes so intent that he felt compelled to face her. "So, why did you come here today? To let me know that you've moved on without me? You're ready to start your new life, which doesn't include me? Is that what you're trying to say? Because if it is, please don't sugarcoat it for me. I'm a big girl. I can handle rejection. Just tell me."

"I don't know. I'm not sure. I'm still trying to figure things out. I'm sorry, Lauren. I came here because Rich told me you were in town. I wanted to see how you were doing, but I'm not ready to decide anything yet. I need more time."

Lauren looked away and put her fists on her hips. "What is there to decide? Do you love me or not?"

Mark took a step toward Lauren and placed his hands on her shoulders. "I do love you, but I'm not sure what is right for the future. Please just give me some more time."

Lauren pulled away from him and turned her attention back to the grill. She turned it off and stacked hamburgers and ribs on a large platter. "I'd better get this food inside. I think everyone's hungry."

Mark followed her inside, where they seemed to get lost in the shuffle of preparations for dinner. Lauren's two sisters made their way outside with bowls of various salads. Lauren gave her mother the platter of meat and then directed each of the children to carry out something to one of the two large picnic tables outside.

Lauren had such a large family that a simple family get-together resembled a full-blown ward activity. It took several minutes for the well-directed troops to bring out all the food and take their places at the table.

Sophie seemed overjoyed to see Mark, and she and Danny each took a seat next to him. Lauren sat directly across from Mark. Her eyes seem to direct themselves in every direction but toward him.

Lauren's father took a few moments to address the family. "I'd like to thank everyone for being here this afternoon, especially Lauren and the kids for coming from so far away. I'd also like to welcome Mark into our midst. It's nice to finally meet you and have you here with us. Most of all, I'd like to express my love for Jacob. I'm so proud of you, son, for all of your accomplishments. We're all happy for you. Although I'm happy about this moment, I have to say I'm a bit saddened because you're the last one to leave our home. I don't think I'm quite ready for an empty nest." He walked over to Jacob and placed a hand on his shoulder. "I love you, son. Congratulations on your graduation." Her father then proceeded to bless the food.

Everyone dug in upon the chorus of amens. Platter after platter was passed around: potato salad, pasta salad, green salad, cucumber salad, three-bean salad, and Jell-O salads of varying colors, along with a variety of chips, rolls, and meat.

Lauren helped Danny and Sophie dish up their food then tore right into hers, devouring an entire plate of ribs. Mark had never seen her eat quite like that before.

He enjoyed the food, along with the company of Lauren's family. Most of her family was friendly and loving, but Rachel seemed a bit outspoken. They were comfortable to be around, making him feel welcome despite Lauren's coolness. He could understand her aloofness; she was upset that he wasn't ready to continue their relationship. Yet for some reason, sitting amongst her family felt right. He could easily see himself becoming a part of this family, but his uneasiness regarding Lauren's past still kept him from committing. It wasn't just her past, though. Thoughts of her career and fortune lingered in his mind and prevented him from going with his heart.

After the meal was finished, the children scurried to play on the swing set while the adults lingered at the tables, conversing. Mark tried to make light conversation with Lauren, but it was obvious she was in no mood to pretend.

"Mark," Lauren hissed, "I really don't know what we're supposed to be saying to each other. I haven't seen you in weeks and you show up on the doorstep. Now we're having dinner together and what are we supposed to be talking about? The weather? Current events? Or how about where have you been all this time? Why are you really here and what on earth am I supposed to expect from you?"

"Please don't be angry," Mark said, reaching across the table for her hand.

"Don't be angry? How can I not be angry?" Lauren's tone clearly indicated just how upset she was. Several of her family members looked over as she raised her voice.

Mark looked away from the curious faces. "I'm sorry."

Lauren pulled her hand out of his grasp and got up from the table. Without another word, she turned away and walked inside the house.

Mark rose from the table and was about to follow her into the house when Rachel came over and pulled him back down. "What do you expect, Mark? She deserves an answer. If you can't accept her for who she is, then move on, but don't keep her hanging like this."

Mark was taken aback by Rachel's forwardness. "I—"

"Leave him alone, Rachel," Rich said walking over to the table where Mark sat. "It's asking a lot for a guy to accept how Lauren's lived her life. She's my sister and I love her, but give the guy a break for not being absolutely sure about this."

"That's fine," Rachel said, turning away from Mark to face Rich. "But, he shouldn't push her away, saying he still loves her, but then he doesn't call her for two weeks. If he can't handle Lauren's success, then maybe he should go find some goody-goody who needs to be taken care of. He shouldn't just keep her hanging on, not knowing."

"Rachel!" Liesel came over, taking a seat next to Mark. "Leave him alone. This is between Mark and Lauren. It is none of your business. You just leave him alone." Liesel turned to Mark. "I'm sorry about my sister, here. She always has to put her two cents in. Don't listen to her. You just do what you think is right—but you should know that Lauren really loves you. She's a wonderful woman, and I know you'd be happy together."

"Liesel, why don't *you* leave the guy alone? I thought this was between Mark and Lauren," Rich said.

"It is. I just want to make sure he knows how much Lauren loves him," Liesel responded.

"He knows," Rich said.

"I know," Mark said, finally feeling like he could say something amidst the discussion among Lauren's siblings. "I know how much she loves me, and I love her too. We're just at a crossroads in our relationship, and I'm trying to figure out what to do next—but you're right, Liesel. This is between Lauren and me. I'm going to go talk to her."

"I think that's a good idea. Talk to her. Don't leave her guessing," Rachel said.

"Leave this poor boy alone," Lauren's mother said, walking over to take his arm. "Come on, I'll show you where Lauren is."

"You're probably upset with me as well," Mark said as he followed her into the house.

"Not upset, just concerned. I'm worried about Lauren and

the kids. From what she tells me, you're a really good man, and I know you'll do the right thing, no matter what it is. Whatever you decide, just make sure your decision is based on what you feel in your heart, not how you think others will judge you." She patted his hand and stopped in front of a closed door down the hall from the living room. "She's in there."

After Lauren's mother walked away, Mark knocked softly on the door. Lauren opened the door and gestured for him to come in. She closed the door. Her eyes were reddened and puffy, and she wiped away a few remaining tears.

Mark caressed her cheek and leaned in to kiss her lips. "I'm so sorry, Lauren. I love you so much and it pains me to see you hurting so much, especially because I know I caused it all."

She shrugged her shoulders and looked away.

"I know it's not fair, but I need more time to figure out my heart. I really love you, but this is not a decision I can take lightly. When I decide what I want in the future, I need to be certain, so there will never be any doubts or regrets. Please trust me, Lauren."

"I just don't know."

"Let's take a few days and really pray about it. What if we go back to Coronado next weekend? That's such a special place for us. It's where I first told you I loved you, but it wasn't the first time I felt it. I love you now more than ever, Lauren, but let's be sure we're ready for the next step."

"Mark, I love you too, but why should we stay apart?"

"Just a week, so we can take time to really pray about it. We have to know this is right for us—and for Danny and Sophie. What do you say, Lauren?" he asked, touching her cheek. "Let's go to Coronado next weekend."

Lauren nodded. "Okay."

Mark embraced Lauren and held her in his arms, wishing it could be easier. He wanted to give her an answer, tell her he wanted to marry her, but it was not that simple. There were still so many issues clouding his ability to make a decision. Hopefully, during the next week, he could take time to pray and go to the temple to seek the answer. He needed to know for a certainty if Lauren was meant to be his wife, his eternal companion.

"I should probably get going," Mark said without releasing her.

Lauren nodded, saying nothing. She pulled away and led the way out of the room. Mark took several minutes to thank Lauren's family for their hospitality. He made sure to have a few words with Danny and Sophie before he left. Both children were saddened to see him go, but he promised it wouldn't be long before he came to visit them. Sophie seemed easily appeased and went back to playing with her cousins. Danny, however, was close to tears and looked down at the ground. Mark looked away, unable to face the pain in his young eyes. It hurt him to see Lauren's reaction as she stood near the gate, waiting for him. She had read Danny's expression and was crushed by it.

Mark hugged Danny and said good-bye to all of Lauren's family, wondering if he would ever see them again. At that moment, he couldn't guess what would happen in the future. There was still so much to resolve in his own mind, and he wasn't sure of the outcome. Lauren led the way to the front of the house, and he stopped her just as they approached his rental car.

"It was good to see you again. I really loved meeting your family."

Lauren nodded, still unable to speak.

"Please don't be angry with me," he said lifting her chin up to meet his eyes.

"It's just so hard."

"I know, but we'll see each other soon."

Lauren shut her eyes and nodded.

Mark embraced Lauren and she clung to him as if she never wanted to let go.

"I love you," Lauren said as she stepped out of his arms. She stood at the end of the driveway and watched as Mark drove away.

20.

When Mark got back to L.A. he drove to Blake's home. Blake was Mark's cousin with whom he'd been staying since he left the garage apartment. Blake owned and operated the Big Spoon, a diner, and was rarely home, so he had been happy to allow Mark to stay there while he sorted through everything. Since he left the Olsens' the day before he'd been unable to think of anything other than Lauren. He still didn't know what to do, but he was certain that he loved her and would find it very difficult—if not impossible—to live without her.

The next day, he decided to go to the temple. He hoped that in the quiet of the celestial room, he might be able to feel the Spirit prompting him as to what to do. He still couldn't put aside his pride as he thought about how much money she made. In his mind, he should be taking care of her and not the other way around.

After the session, he sat in quietude, pondering the overwhelming decision he needed to make. As he thought back on their relationship, he tried to remember what had attracted him to her.

She was a loving woman, and he had always marveled at how she had raised two well-behaved and caring children without a husband. All that Danny and Sophie were could be attributed to Lauren; none of it came from their fathers. Her ability to independently raise two children impressed him—why then did he hold that independence against her? He thought back to the time he had driven her and Sophie to the hospital. Lauren had been so scared of losing Sophie and he remembered being able to comfort her. He'd liked feeling needed and had really enjoyed the look of appreciation in Lauren's eyes.

As he thought back to other times when he had been able to provide comfort or support to Lauren, he realized she did need him. Perhaps she didn't need his money, but did that really matter? He had so much more to offer her than money. Why couldn't that be enough for him? It was enough for her. Mark closed his eyes and tried to imagine life without her. He needed her too. Mark thought about their upcoming date and realized he couldn't wait to see Lauren again. All other doubts that had once seemed all-encompassing were gone. The one-time belief that it was an impossible love was replaced by a certitude that this love was meant to be. Nothing else, not even the past, mattered.

Lauren went back to California and attempted to fall back into her routine, but constant thoughts of Mark left her unable to concentrate on much else. She was anxious to see him again, but at the same time worried that the next time she saw him would be the last. She had been dumped before—plenty of times—but this one would hurt more than any of the others.

Mark had been true love; the others had been a fleeting sort of fanciful and artificial love that didn't truly mean anything.

She would be seeing him in a few days and wondered what was going to happen. He hadn't given her any sign to make her feel that there was hope. Should she have any hope? They would be going back to Coronado. There were so many good memories there, and the fact that he wanted to take her there did give her a small degree of hope. As she finished reading her scriptures, she hesitated before turning to prayer. Lauren lay on her bed and pondered why this was happening to her. She had come a long way, changed her life in so many ways, and felt she was finally on the correct path that would lead her to eternal happiness. Mark had come into her life at the precise moment when she had realized she needed to change her life in order to secure true happiness. Now that she had come back to living the gospel, it seemed like a cruel twist of fate that she would not have Mark in her life. Didn't she deserve him? Didn't she deserve to be happy now that she had repented and was working toward living righteously?

With tear-filled eyes and a heavy heart, she pulled herself out of bed, dropped to her knees, and prayed. She asked Heavenly Father all those questions. Didn't she deserve true happiness now? Was it possible that Mark was being taken away from her at the exact moment she had changed her life? As she got back onto her bed, she pondered these questions. Although it didn't seem fair, the more she thought about it, a sense of understanding seemed to unfold. Mark had come into her life during a time when she had been spiraling out of control. She'd just lost her license for driving drunk. Only now could she admit that she did have a drinking problem. She'd also been chasing men, like Julian, who were worthless. It took Mark coming into her life to make her realize that she wanted, and even deserved, to have someone better than Julian or the long list of shallow men she'd dated.

Perhaps that had been Mark's purpose. Was it possible that Heavenly Father had put Mark in her path to help her realize her value and aid her in returning to His fold? Now that she had accepted the gospel in her life once again, would he move on? She shuddered to think about it. She truly loved Mark and wanted to be his wife. As she pulled her blanket over her, she realized that whatever Heavenly Father had planned for her, she would accept it. No matter how much she loved Mark and wanted him in her life, Heavenly Father had a plan for her. She hoped it included Mark, but knew that she would survive if it didn't. She could stand on her own two feet and felt confident that she would never stray from the gospel again.

Nevertheless, she was still in love with Mark. She knew she would do everything in her power to be with him and gladly give up any material possession she had. Only recently had she realized that money didn't bring her true happiness. Danny and Sophie were the most important aspects of her life, and apart from them she would give up anything. She now knew she was willing to do whatever it took to be with Mark, but even if things didn't work out, she would always be thankful for the role he played in helping her find her way.

The next morning, she winced when her alarm went off. It was four in the morning; she could never think clearly that early in the morning. Her stomach was doing somersaults as she prepared for the day. She was being interviewed by a national early-morning news show. As was customary prior to an interview, Lauren was feeling out of sorts and nervous.

As the limo driver pulled up in front of the studio, Lauren said a silent prayer that her interview would go well and that her nerves would be calm. Today's interview was particularly nerve-racking because she had been in the news a lot lately. As a recent Oscar winner, she had become a highly sought after actress who was being offered parts by many high-powered producers. What had set her apart from many Oscar award-winning actresses who came before was the fact that she was turning down nearly every proffered script.

As she read through the scripts that were pouring in, Lauren realized there were few roles she would consider taking. Most of the movies being made contained graphic and provocative material that she wouldn't want to see come to screen, much less be involved in herself. The parts being thrown her way contained profanity and sexual situations, and she was turning down script after script. Her agent and manager were barely on speaking terms with her. Both men were outraged at her inability to look past the offensive material by accepting parts that were sure to garner her—and in turn them—future success.

The rumor mill of Hollywood had been churning as word spread that Lauren Olsen thought she was too good to accept parts from award-winning directors and producers. She was being blacklisted in Hollywood. She was now ready to face her accusers and stand up for herself and her principles.

Lauren knew she was losing her hold on Hollywood, but it didn't matter. For the first time in her life, her career wasn't her main focus. There were facets of her life that carried so much more importance than her next role. Over the past weeks, she'd had a lot of time to think, and she had made several decisions concerning her life. Whether Mark came back into her life or not, Lauren was clear about certain changes that were going to take place. As she reminded herself of the significant blessings present in her life, the magnitude of the interview seemed to lessen.

The interview started off casually enough. The veteran morning news anchor, Leslie Maynes, who was beloved by the entire country, began the interview by congratulating Lauren on her recent success.

"Tell me, Lauren, how has winning an Oscar changed you?"

"Well, the actual award hasn't really changed me. I had been in a process of change before the Oscars. I had been reexamining my values and belief system, trying to make changes in my life that would bring my children and me greater happiness."

Leslie smiled what seemed to Lauren a fake smile. "I've heard from several people in the business that you are turning down many excellent scripts. Why is that?"

Lauren explained her upbringing. She went on to give intimate details of her life, how she had ventured so far from her religious beliefs. "I've made life-altering decisions in the past year and am prepared to stand by them. I no longer believe in accepting roles that are overly profane or explicit, nor will I be involved in films that would most likely garner an R rating."

"Don't you agree that filmmakers have a right to express themselves?"

"Of course they have a right to express themselves—and I have a right to refuse to work on a film that I believe is offensive."

"But sometimes the subject matter is innately offensive. If a producer wants to make a film about a harsh reality of life, is it okay to sugarcoat it just so you are not offended?"

"What I am saying is that stories can be told without overdoing it. *West Side Story* tells about the lives of gang members without having to use four letter words. It can be done in an inoffensive manner and still make a powerful statement. However, I am not saying that filmmakers need to conform to my standards. I am simply saying that I no longer wish to participate in films that push the envelope."

Leslie smiled a mischievous smile, ready for an intense conversation. "Well, you've made films in the past that were R-rated—why the sudden change?"

"My priorities have changed. I used to want to be admired as an actress by my peers. I wanted to be an A-list actress. Now, the only thing that matters is that I have the admiration of my children. I want my kids to be proud of me for living according to my standards. I want to be able to go to sleep at night knowing I didn't participate in the infectious onslaught of violent and profane films our children are subjected to.

"Children are desensitized at such a young age now. There are kids in my children's grades, kindergarten and first grade, who regularly watch R-rated movies. The violence and sexuality young children witness on a daily basis will clearly make an impact on their future behavior. Hollywood needs to be made accountable for that, and I no longer wish to be a part of that."

"Months ago, there was some talk in the tabloids about your involvement with your chauffeur. Does he have anything to do with your new way of thinking?"

"In part, maybe. These are standards I was raised with, standards I didn't live by for some time, but I do believe in them. He also shares these beliefs and his friendship has helped me want to live that way again."

"So, you're doing all of *this* for a man?" Leslie asked.

Lauren laughed. "No, not for a man. For myself and for my children. I am doing *this* because I believe it's what is right. But, if there is one thing I learned in all of this, it's that there are more important things than good roles, or careers, or Oscars. There is something altogether more important—and that is a powerful, eternal love that you can't even fathom unless you've felt it yourself. I'm talking about a love that can overcome anything. A love that is so right that you know God is looking down, smiling. A love that knows no pride or envy. It is a pure and everlasting love that can't be equaled. That is the kind of love that I have for this man.

"And so you ask me, am I doing all this for a man. The answer is no. I'm not doing this for him, but if I were, there would be nothing wrong with that. Because the love I feel for him surpasses any kind of happiness I could obtain from making movies. I would gladly give it all up if he asked me to. That's what you want me to say, right? You guys are all the same. You ask the same questions and want the same titillating answers. Well, there you have it. Just so there's no misunderstanding. Yes, I am in love with my chauffeur and I would give up every material thing I have—my house, my career, everything—if he asked me to."

Leslie had little more to say after Lauren's concluding statements. After the interview was wrapped up, there was also very little to say as Lauren was excused from the set and escorted back to her limo.

As the door of the limo closed, she sat back and sighed heavily. It all still felt like a blur. Had she really said all those things to Leslie? Was it really being televised live all over the country? The instant ringing of the phone told her it was. An onslaught of phone calls from her manager, agent, and publicist informed her she had just committed career suicide. What had she been thinking? Why had she bad-mouthed the hand that had fed her for so long? Did she want to ever work in this town again? Lauren didn't care what any of them said. She stood by her statement; she would gladly give up her career and all her money if Mark asked her to.

Her cell phone rang again and Lauren prepared herself to defend her actions again. "What?" she asked.

"I would never ask you to," said a gentle voice that Lauren recognized as Mark's.

"Mark?"

"Hi."

"You saw my interview?" she asked.

"Yes and I would never ask you to give all that up. You've worked so hard for it."

"None of it means anything to me without you. Where are you, Mark?"

"I'm at a pay phone on Santa Monica Boulevard. I'd been watching the show at a diner my cousin owns. Where are you?"

"We just left the studio. I think we're about to get on the 101."

"Get off on Santa Monica Boulevard. I want to see you," Mark said, giving her the address to the diner.

Lauren gave the instructions to the limo driver and held her breath in anticipation of seeing Mark again. It seemed like a lifetime since she'd last seen him.

It was only a matter of minutes before they pulled up next to Mark's car. He was standing outside the Nissan, hands deep in the pockets of his jeans. Lauren thought she saw anticipation in his eyes, but it couldn't equal the eagerness she felt at seeing him again. Lauren stepped out of the limo and the driver closed the door.

She approached Mark, clasping her hands together, trying to wipe off the sweat. "Hi, there," she said, never remembering feeling this nervous.

"You look beautiful," Mark said, approaching her. He hesitated for only a moment before taking her into his arms. He held her tightly against him and buried his face in her hair. "I love you so much. I'm sorry for how I behaved."

Lauren's tension eased away as she felt herself melting into his embrace. Nothing else seemed to matter at that moment except for the fact that he loved her. "I've missed you so much," she said to him.

Mark pulled himself away, but still held her close. "Can you send the limo driver away? I'll take you home."

Lauren obliged, pulling herself away from Mark only long enough to speak to the limo driver and retrieve her handbag, which she put on the roof of Mark's car.

She walked right back into Mark's waiting arms. He looked at her for only a moment before he kissed her. "I'm sorry I wasted so much time. I was so foolish, so full of pride. Can you forgive me?"

"You really hurt me, Mark. I can't go on the way things have been." She paused, not wanting to ask her next question. "How do you feel about things now?"

"I love you, Lauren. I want to be with you. Nothing else matters." He reached into his front pocket and slowly pulled out something. He held her hand and showed her a ring. Lauren gasped, bringing her hand up to cover her mouth. It was a thin gold band that held a small diamond. A little ring, by comparison to her previous ones, but it didn't matter. The larger, more expensive diamond rings from her two other marriages seemed small, insignificant when compared to the immense significance of this one. This small ring signified eternal love. "I want to marry you," he said.

It was what she had been hoping for, praying for almost from the instant she'd met him. He was saying the words she had dreamt of for so long. Lauren looked at the ring, wondering when he'd picked it out. How long had he had it? "I want to marry you," she repeated, looking up to meet his eyes.

He took her hand and slid the ring onto her finger. "I bought this ring a few months ago. I was waiting for the right time to ask and then that stupid tabloid came out and I couldn't think straight. I'm sorry I doubted you. Most of all, I'm sorry I hurt you. You didn't deserve that. But I promise you I will never doubt you again. I love you for who you are, and I want to be with you forever."

Lauren closed her eyes, hoping that when she opened them it wouldn't just be a dream. Before she could open her eyes, Mark was kissing her eyelids softly, wiping away the tears of happiness that had overwhelmed her. When she opened her eyes again, Mark was still there and his love for her was evident in his smiling eyes.

"I love Danny and Sophie. I want to be the father they deserve. I hope I can adopt them and we can have them sealed to us. I really want us to be a family. Do you think their fathers will object?"

Lauren shook her head. "I don't think that will be a problem. I can't think of anything I would like more than that. I know Danny and Sophie will be so happy. They really love you."

Mark smiled. "Let's go tell them."

"Before we go, there are some things I want to tell you. I've had a lot of time to think these past few weeks and I've made some decisions. First of all, I'm going to sell the house. It'll go on the market on Monday. It's too much. I want something smaller. And now that we're getting married, I think it should be something we pick out together."

Mark smiled. "I'd like that. A three-bedroom house—just enough for us."

"Well, maybe four or five bedrooms. We're going to need more room for the babies."

"Babies?" Mark asked with a smile.

Lauren nodded. "Don't you want babies?"

He smiled again. "Of course, I want babies. I can't wait to have babies with you."

"I'm also going to stop acting for a while once this movie's done. I'll still review scripts from time to time, but I'm only going to do a film if I feel really strongly about it and if it sends the right kind of message. I would like to start a production company and begin developing projects myself.

"Rather than turn my back on the industry, I think I should use this mechanism to make a statement. There are many moviegoers who are tired of blockbusters filled with violence, nudity, and profanity. I really think there is an audience that would appreciate a movie that sends a positive message. There are stories that need to be told and a certain way they need to be told. I may just be one person, but I think I can make a difference, even if it is a little one. What do you think about me starting a production company?"

"I think you should do it. I know you would succeed in anything you tried. You have a gift, Lauren, that transcends the screen. You have a voice and a foothold on this business that can make a difference. I know so many people who have almost given up on going to the movies because of all the trash they put out. You're right, there is an audience craving wholesome entertainment. I would whole-heartedly support you on this. All I ask is no more kissing scenes for you," he said, half-joking, but Lauren knew he was quite serious.

"No more kissing scenes. I think I'd like to work in the background for a while, but when I do go back to acting, I promise you can read through the whole script and help me decide."

Mark smiled and kissed her again. "I'm really proud of you for all these decisions you made. I know we're going to be very happy. I can't wait to be married."

"So, what about you? Did you decide on a job?"

Mark nodded. "The law firm I clerked with all through

college has offered me a position. I already told them I would take it. So, I plan on staying put."

"Good," Lauren said. "Let's go home and tell our kids about the wedding. They've really missed you."

"Our kids," Mark said with a smile. "I really like the sound of that." Mark opened the passenger side door and kissed Lauren one more time before helping her inside.

He went around to his side and held her hand tightly as they drove home. Lauren felt so happy. They were finally going to be the family she had envisioned so many times. At that moment, she knew she could conquer anything with Mark at her side.

21

Two years later

Mark sat nervously holding Lauren's hand in his. It was exactly three years ago that he'd sat in the Kodak Theater in awe of his surroundings. Once again, he was in awe, but the shimmering lights overhead and the glamorous movie stars around him were not what impressed him. It was the extraordinary woman seated next to him who had earned his admiration.

As she squeezed his hand, Mark couldn't imagine loving Lauren any more. She had triumphed despite being shunned in an industry that had once held her in high esteem. Lauren was not popular among the peers who had once lauded her, but despite the many attempts to stand in her way of producing films, she had come up on top. She had done what she'd set out to do, working against their rules and holding fast to her standards along the way.

Mark's mind wandered during the presentation of the Best Actress award and within minutes, his attention was once again captivated. A renowned Hollywood director took his place on center stage and read off the list of nominated films, concluding the ceremony by presenting the Oscar for Best Picture. "And the Oscar goes to *The Hiding Place,* executive producer Lauren Olsen Ellege."

The announcement was followed by applause as the Oscar was awarded to the little independent film Lauren's company had produced. It had been a David against a mass of Goliaths— films that had been produced by the major studios of Hollywood. Mark jumped to his feet and helped Lauren up. He kissed her and then began applauding harder than he ever had. Lauren had taken the story of Corrie and Betsie ten Boom, Dutch women who had risked their lives to help hide Jews from the Nazis.

Lauren walked up to the microphone and was followed by an entourage of people—producers, directors, actors, and an ensemble from the film. "Going up those stairs is hard enough without being eight and a half months pregnant," Lauren said as the audience laughed. She took a deep breath and then continued. "It was truly an honor to be able to make this film. Betsie and Corrie ten Boom are an inspiration to me. In honoring me with this award, you are honoring them.

"Several years ago, I made a promise to myself that I would never be involved in a film that I would be uncomfortable having my children watch. This award is proof that you can make a film that is exceptional and inspirational without being overly provocative or profane. A film can be uplifting and still have something important to say, without having to be offensive. I am forever grateful to the entire cast and crew who worked extraordinarily hard on the making of this film."

Lauren went on to specifically name the starring actresses and director. She also mentioned several of the people from her production company. "I would like to say thank you to my son, Danny, who with the simple question of a six-year-old, challenged me and inspired me to change my life. To my daughter, Sophie, thank you for demonstrating what it truly means to be a daughter of God. I'm grateful for a family that never stopped loving me and never stopped praying for me. Thank you to my wonderful husband, Mark, for your complete support and love. Almost from the instant I met you, you have inspired me to be a better person. I love you so much. Thank you to the Academy for the wonderful honor."

After Lauren finished her acceptance speech, she waddled offstage, having never looked more beautiful. The gown she wore had been specially made for her to fit her very pregnant body. It seemed like forever before Lauren was released by the press and she joined Mark.

Once in the privacy of the limo, Mark pulled Lauren into an embrace. It was in similar circumstances that he had first realized he loved Lauren. Now, more than ever, he was convinced that loving Lauren was what Heavenly Father had always intended for him. It had just taken Mark a little longer to realize it.

About the Author

Marcia Argueta Mickelson was born in Guatemala but grew up mostly in New Jersey. In high school, she started writing her first novel, which she didn't finish until ten years later. She followed her sister to Brigham Young University, where she met her husband, Nolan. Marcia received her degree in American studies. Upon graduating, she began working for a nonprofit organization in Salt Lake City. She ran a foster care program that helped place children in foster homes, trained foster parents, and provided mentoring services for children.

When Nolan graduated, Marcia persuaded him to move to New Jersey, where they started a family. Now they live in San Antonio, Texas, with their three sons: Omar, Diego, and Ruben.

About the Author ✶⭑˙✛✳˓✛✶✻˙⭑

Marcia is a stay-at-home mom who substitute teaches in local elementary schools, spending most of her nights in front of the computer, writing. She is the Primary president of her ward. When she's not busy with mothering, writing, and Primary, she enjoys reading books, seeing movies, working on scrapbooks, and watching BYU football games with her husband.

Marcia would love to hear from her readers. She can be e-mailed at *marcia_mickelson@yahoo.com*.